Lily and Blue

Lily and Blue

barbara j. weigel

Cover Design by Tor Anderson

ISBN: 978-1-66783-695-9

—

*This book is dedicated
to the animals and humans
who have been unloved and abused,
and to the people who help to rescue them.*

*And to Lillian Juniper Jade Weigel,
who is very well loved and cared for.
May she grow up with an abiding love
of the natural world and all its creatures.*

CONTENTS

*Not until we are lost do we begin
to understand ourselves.*

—*Henry David Thoreau*

The more I wonder, the more I love.

—*Alice Walker,* The Color Purple

Prologue

Starting in the middle, but soon backtracking to the beginning and finishing at the end, this is the account of Lily's and Blue's life together.

Depending upon your own travels, you may have seen these two wandering the verdant hills, gentle rivers and sunlit beaches of central California. Maybe you joined them as you hiked along a mountain trail east of The Angels, known to most as Los Angeles. Perhaps you met them exploring the high desert mesas and red rock canyons of Taos and the Southwest. Did you place money in their open guitar case as they sang and entertained you on the small-town streets of Santa Cruz? You might know them well, or not at all. Either way, this is their story.

The Middle

BLUE

The first rays of sun sneak through the netted door of our tent. I can smell the early morning moisture of the wild grasses just outside. It is clear that deer have nosed around our sleep spot a few hours before, though I was tired and slept through their passing. A horn beeps in the distance and I smell coffee roasting farther away.

My body, warm from Lily sleeping next to me, eases into a long stretch. I am stiff again and my hips are a dull reminder that I no longer can do the acrobatic moves that once made us a good living. These days, when Lily and I work the streets I wear bits of costume, tilting my head in cute gestures and shaking hands with people. I don't care if I need to appear the clown as long as I am close to Lily.

I haven't had a burger or hot dog for two days, and I want one. My mouth waters just thinking about the last burger Lily bought for me.

As she crawls out from under the quilts, Lily grabs a few perforated squares of paper towel. She sings my name as she holds my face. Then she is off to find a hidden place to go take a dump. A few years ago, Lily confided that she preferred doing her business in the fields and bushes and under the trees, as long as she didn't see anybody. I join her to find my own place to relieve myself, and to keep an eye on her.

Done with our business, Lily and I step back into the tent, where she feeds me treats and writes in her journal. Absentmindedly she touches my head and ears a few times as I snuggle close to her. She smells like the beach and smoke from the fire pit last night. Hopping up, she gets fully dressed and says, "Time to pack up, buddy."

Singing my favorite song about love, a river, a flower, and me being a seed, we take down Big Alice, our tent, and walk up the small hillside to our rolling home, Homer. Lily loves our car and I do too. She loads the tent along with our nighttime belongings through Homer's back lift-up window.

I start to get in when Lily says, "Come on, let's walk to the gas station to clean up, then we'll get coffee and treats. It's just a few blocks and Homer seems happy to be right where she is." I fall into pace beside Lily.

. . . .

As they walk to the gas station, Lily watches Blue move stiffly and thinks, *I'll have to get him more baby aspirin before work today, his arthritis seems to be bothering him.* Visiting Santa Cruz now, Lily remembers what she and Blue went through when they lived here before. Bending down to hug him, she says out loud, "Blue, you are not allowed to get any older. You need to stay with me forever." She takes a breath. "How about a burger this afternoon, my little prince of princes, my king of kings? It's been a couple of days." Blue looks at Lily and smiles his goofy dog smile. Lily laughs.

Lightly holding Blue's leash, Lily hums softly as she glimpses the silver sparkle of reflection floating just above the pavement. Few people are on the street, the sun is warm, and as Lily tilts her head to look up at the flawless light-blue sky, she sees a still-lingering, neatly sliced half moon hanging upside down, an omen of something, but she does not know what.

At the gas station bits of graffiti adorn the walls, telling any who enter that this is a public urinal. Blue's coat is looking a bit ragged, and when Lily looks in the mirror, so is she. Her long blond hair is a saltwater mass of tangles and there is dirt smudged on her sleepy face. Looking closely in the mirror and not seeing any pimples she needs to pick, Lily chirps to Blue, "This bathroom clean-up should do us okay for today."

Blue is a stocky pit bull and Lily knows it's important for him to look cute for the public. Mostly white with black eye, forehead, torso and rump patches, Blue is a handsome dog. Some people are afraid of him, as some people think all pits are scary. It's true that Blue has a large head, wide pit bull jaw, muscular body, and the neck scars he got as a puppy, but he is as gentle and smart as any dog could be. Lily puts on his "cute dog" turquoise bandana for now. When they return from breakfast, before they start their gig, she will dress him in his little cowboy vest, currently packed in Homer.

In the old days of working on the street, Blue was able to jump against a tree or the side of a building and do backflips, but now he is relegated to a dog clown act, shaking people's hands and howling along with parts of her songs. He brings in most of the tips and Lily knows it. She looks at Blue and giggles as he puffs out his chest and struts down the sidewalk towards the coffee shop. She calls out, "Hey, Hambone, wait for me!"

The Beginning

"NO!" exclaims Lily.

When other students in class look at her, Lily catches herself daydreaming again and realizes that her voice went public. Sheepishly she smiles, then silently continues ruminating. *College is not for me, I say NO to another day of boredom, it's almost been a year. It's not inspiring, it's soul destructive. I can't keep faking my life. I say No to college, No to city concrete, No to too many people, too many cars and too much human noise.*

As soon as class is over, Lily grabs her books and backpack and heads out the door. No goodbye, no gotta go, this exit is final. She runs through the hall, pushes the door handle hard, skips down the steps, and as she runs across the lawn to her car, she happily exclaims, "Fuck it!"

Safely ensconced in her dusty Subaru wagon, her freedom machine, Lily bangs her palms on the steering wheel. She tilts the rearview mirror down to see her face and asks, "What am I doing? Who am I?" Looking at herself, she laughs. "I have no clue."

The seats are hot and her legs stick to the fake leather. She puts the key in the ignition, rolls down the windows, turns on the radio and hears U2 howling, "I wanna run, I want to hide. I wanna tear down the walls that hold me inside."

Shocked that this song is on the radio at this moment, she cranks the sound and joins in at the top of her lungs, "I wanna reach out and touch the flame, where the streets have no name.'"

The year is 2003 and Lily, at nineteen, yearns for something. Her *whys* and *whats* are endless. If she said her truth out loud, she would say that she wants the elements of earth and sky to work their way into her, to teach her, bend her, train her to become a part of whatever there is to be a part of. She'd talk of a wildness, an unknown that lives deep inside her, a feral trait, as if there were a pack of wild dogs racing through her veins.

Right then and there, Lily decides she will go where the streets have no name, that she will experience her own walkabout. An avid reader, Lily has studied the practice of the Aboriginal walkabout. It's time for her own rite of passage, her walk to survive, a time of isolation and deep thought.

Driving home to Norma's, she smells the diesel trucks roaring past and sighs. She will leave in a few days. She won't tell her dad, who is living somewhere with his latest chosen female grad student, and he probably wouldn't notice anyway. She wonders if her birth mother or her stepmother will protect her from the other side. They both have been dead for years. Lily has this idea that the dead who couldn't love on earth learn to love as spirits. The only real love she's ever felt is from Norma, her neighbor, whom she has been living with since she was fifteen. Lily knows she would be dead by now if it weren't for Norma.

Hopping out of the car, Lily slows to inhale the sweet fragrance of the pale pink and golden heirloom roses Norma has planted along the front garden path. A nature girl at heart, Lily is an odd combination of old soul and instinctive child. A bit unkempt, her long blond hair hangs tangled and free, and her well-used clothes are hastily thrown on. Unsettled, unconventional and independent, she is inextricably woven of soil, trees, rivers and mountains, a loner floating through the world, trying to figure out where her feet belong. Scared to be off on her own, Lily thinks her survival depends on allowing herself to be lost, to feel that wolf at the door, and if necessary, to invite her in.

Lily's First Walkabout

Curious chipmunks greet Lily at every turn, reminding her of the childhood backyard squirrels who would scamper this way and that, endlessly entertaining her. It is mid-spring as Lily begins her walkabout on the trails of the San Gabriel Mountains. These peaks and valleys are a natural partition that prohibits the City of Angels from floating down into the Mojave Desert.

The lower hills are dry and dusty and covered with loud humans. Kids are running and shouting while their parents bark commands to be careful. A young boy is throwing rocks at a chipmunk. Lily is infuriated. She can't decide whether to tell him that these creatures are in their home, that humans are the visitors and need to respect them, or to throw a rock at this total brat. She does neither, as his parents are nearby and laughing at their son's antics.

Shaking her head in disgust, Lily says loudly to the parents, "Why are you laughing? That's not cute, it's mean."

It takes her the better part of the day to escape the tourist crowds. The air is hot and thinning as she climbs, her breathing labored and her fifty-pound backpack digging into her shoulders. Lily loves every bit of this, the discomfort of her body and the silence which is not silent at all, as her ears catch the rustle of the wind in the trees. Trudging by, she says hello to the gossiping chipmunks, imperious blue jays, and the stark beige lizards sunning on rocks and decaying tree trunks.

After having read quite a few wilderness and camping manuals, Lily brought only the essentials. She has worn-in hiking boots from her weekly hikes in Griffith Park and in Fryman and Malibu Canyons. Her pack is stuffed full of dried food, a small cookstove, water purification pills, a water bottle, small tent and sleeping bag, a change of clothes, four pairs of socks, flashlight and batteries, matches, plastic bags, poop shovel, a serious knife, a small pot and pan, a mug, dish, fork, and spoon, toilet paper, biodegradable soap, tampons, a few condoms just in case, and most importantly tea, hot chocolate packets, paper and pen. Norma bought her a Gore-Tex jacket and long johns for chilly nights. She is worried about Lily's hastily decided adventure but she kept quiet. Lily would come home when ready.

On the third day, after not seeing another human for hours, Lily begins to shed her suburban skin. Except for socks and hiking boots, she lies naked, sunny side down, heating herself on a large, flat granite slab. Her heartbeat is in tune with the beat of rock and earth, her mind drifting in and out of sunbaked dreams.

A switch of movement is followed by a swooshing rattle, an unmistakable sound. Lily directs her gaze to see the beige-brown diamond pattern of a rattlesnake poised just below. Lying extremely still and holding her breath, she silently counts *one…two…* When the count gets to seven, she sighs as the snake slithers away. She stretches her heat-flushed body to shake off jangled nerves. Worried that other rattlers are hiding nearby, she carefully creeps around the rock outcropping, double-inspecting cracks and crevices. All looks safe, so she hops back onto the granite bed, positioning herself on her back. Her thoughts are as cloudless as the clear cobalt sky above the snowcapped mountains. Hours of pine and cedar scent drift along the slight breeze. Dressing again, Lily grabs her pack, chugs water, and continues her climb up the trail.

Over the next many days, Lily finds herself stripping down her attire until she is walking almost naked. She wears only socks and boots, a baseball cap, and an unbuttoned plaid shirt so her backpack doesn't irritate her skin. She loves the sound of her boots crunching the dry, rocky soil, interrupted only by the chirp of birds and crickets. As she marches along, she sings made-up songs to the robins and jays and tells little stories to the brush rabbits and other creatures that cross her path. Lily feels happier than she has felt in years, maybe ever.

A red-tailed hawk swoops low and fast between ponderosa and Jeffrey pines, eyeing a late afternoon snack below. Lily stops to watch, breathing in the sweet butterscotch pine scent, but doesn't see if the hawk catches anyone. Another day she hears the hollow sound of woodpeckers knocking against beetle-devoured tree trunks, their gray, white, and red bodies doing a poor job of camouflage. Two large and hand-some Steller's jays, dressed in their brilliant blue uniforms, come sweeping in to grab the insects they want. It's a bully battle between the jays and the woodpeckers. Lily doesn't know which team to root for, but figures there are enough bugs to satisfy both.

At the muddy edge of a slow-moving part of a stream, there are large fresh paw prints that Lily is sure belong to a mountain lion. She looks all around, ex-cited to see one of California's great cougars, but lions, like bears, would rather not encounter humans. She's in agreement with them; she doesn't want to see other humans either.

Since there are no other signs of the lion, she stops to watch frogs and clusters of polliwogs being themselves, swimming, hopping and zigzagging in the shallows between rocks and waterlogged branches. Removing her boots, socks, and clothes, Lily joins them in the melted snow runoff. The water's rippling and rumbling sounds hold earth's memories and secrets as it roller-coasters down the granite peaks, pulling bits of rock and soil with it. She relaxes on the pebbly dirt floor of the stream, her knees and nose acting as landing fields for a few flies who want nothing but a short investigation of her.

Blistered and healed again, Lily's feet are well initiated. Her nose peels no matter how often she slathers on the lemony scented SPF 30. The sting of sweat dripping down into her eyes is a daily ritual. Tan all over, her back and leg muscles have become strong. She enjoys wandering this twenty-two mile wide, sixty-eight mile long mountain range in isolation, from the sage-scented chaparral to granite peaks above the tree line and back again. She covers miles of the Pacific Crest Trail, Mt. Baldy, Devil's Backbone and Copper Canyon, and even explores the more touristed places of Ice House Canyon and Hermit Falls. Quite adept now, she knows how to pack lightly, where to place her tent, which people to avoid and who to chat with. Mule deer feel comfortable coming close to her, and when black bears steal her food, she is reminded that she is in their territory, camping on their land.

Clothing becomes a must as the weeks gather to the end of June. Day hikers in twos and threes and Pacific Crest Trail aficionados are taking over the mountains and canyons. Her wild friends begin to hide from the humans. Lily enjoys sharing food and stories with some of the respectful travelers. The tourists, however, are loud and unaware of the animals' needs and leave garbage at their campsites. Once again feeling the outsider, Lily circles her last campsite, touching the boulders and trees, twirling her body in the warm air. "Time to move on. Thank you dear mountains of San Gabriel for welcoming me."

At sunset the sky is a brilliant golden orange, like a heavenly sky cathedral where the spirits sing your name. It's the kind of sunset that can break your heart wide open. Lily lies back on the hard-packed earth and stares up at the intense starlit sky. Luminously scrawled across the heavens, the Milky Way is a flashlight highway right above her eyes. The depth of darkness between each spot of light is mystical and vast, as shooting stars speed to unknown destinations.

The Bookstore Guy

Taking only the back roads while heading southeast, Lily thinks about the past weeks. She has loved her solo time on the land, but her walkabout has not healed her hurting heart. Norma told her a few years ago to trust her own life, but she still does not know what that means. A longtime elementary school teacher, Norma once told Lily, "Children who have not been loved enough, or in the right way, can take a long time to learn to love themselves. You are one of those children. You're a survivor and will learn, but you must be patient."

Most of the time Lily just feels emotionally numb, like there's a steel force field protecting her heart. Her independence and spontaneity push her and keep her going.

After a few hours, Homer delivers Lily to a funky little hill town in the San Jacinto Mountains called Idyllwild. At first glance she sees it's a mix of laid-back counterculture arty types and elderly retirees. She's ready to stay a night or two in a motel and has enough money from Mother's monthly trust payments to indulge herself.

At the motel Lily luxuriates in a long, hot bath, washes her hair and puts on clean clothes. She hops in Homer to drive the few blocks into town, where she loads her car with easy pack food, more flashlight batteries, water purifying tablets and toilet paper. At the bookstore she buys three paperbacks: a picture book of local flora and fauna, a local trail map pamphlet, and *Refuge*, a book by Terry Tempest Williams. Driving back to the motel, she dumps everything on a chair and walks back to town to a restaurant bar.

Menu in hand, she orders cheesy French bread and a salad with vinaigrette. When the bread arrives at her table, she wolfs down the rich melted cheddar and salted herb bread. Wiping the oil from her lips with a paper napkin, she orders another. The dinner salad is nothing special, but in that moment the cold crunch of fresh lettuce is heaven. She would love a beer or something harder but she's not twenty-one and doesn't have a fake ID. Finished with dinner and delving into the new flora and fauna book, she notices the guy from the bookstore walk into the restaurant. He sees her and comes over uninvited to sit at her table.

"Hi, I'm Ben, and that's a good book," he says, pointing to the naturalist book in her hands.

"Hmm," responds Lily.

"Wanna beer?" he asks.

"You read my mind, but I'm not of age."

"No worries, I am, and I know the bartender. What kind?"

"Sierra Nevada with a shot of tequila," Lily says with a smile.

Ben comes back with the same for himself and begins telling Lily all about the town, and how he moved from Chicago two years before to take a ceramics workshop and stayed.

Lily interrupts, "You sure talk a lot."

"That's what people say." He continues, "Idyllwild is like a weird little village of old folks, potheads, artists and tourists. I like it here, beats living in the Big Windy."

Looking at him, half listening to his saga, Lily thinks he's okay. Kind of cute and super tall, with an East Coast, dark curly hair preppie look mixed with semi-Western horsiness. As the night proceeds with more beer and more tequila, more laughter and flirting, he becomes much cuter. Ben offers to walk Lily to the motel and proceeds to help himself into her room.

In the morning, after what Lily thinks was very adequate and much-needed on-again, off-again, all-night sex, Ben offers to treat her to breakfast. Lily grabs the book of maps, and as they walk to the local greasy spoon, he continues their conversation of the night before about local hiking and camping.

Lily orders scrambled eggs and toast. Ben hems and haws while trying to decide, finally settling on oatmeal with bananas, and coffee for both of them. She is bit turned off by his indecisiveness but asks if he wants to take a day hike with her. He has a few days off from the bookstore, so they agree to backpack together for the next three days. Lily likes the idea of going with someone who knows the special places to explore. One of the area landmarks is called Lily Rock, a popular destination for rock climbers, but as Lily is not a climber, she is only interested in where to get the best close-up view.

As they begin their hike, Lily scours the flora and fauna book for names of the local trees and certain shrubs. Manzanita and coyote brush are everywhere, and there are surprise treats like incense cedar, white alder, and the Coulter pine with its large, golden-beige cones. Ferns sprout from shady crevices along the river's edge. Lily enjoys the landscape more than she enjoys Ben's need to talk. Intermittently she wanders off by herself for much-needed quiet time. Ben's not catching on that his river of words is irritating, and she considers that this is why she travels solo. Having sex is nice but not quite worth the constant verbal diarrhea.

On their last day together, Ben offers to show Lily next spring's spectacular beauty, when the hills are covered with purple and gold flowers. Lily changes the subject.

As the sun slides behind the mountain, a fluttering sound fills the air and a horde of bats arrive, skirting and darting every which way. The mosquitos have been fierce and the bats know exactly where to find their food. Lily sits quietly in awe, as Ben crawls into the tent and waits fearfully until the dark takes hold and the bats move on.

'Shrooms

After returning to town and thanking Ben, Lily is ready to venture solo again. She cruises down through the lower elevations and dry, rolling hills of Julian and the remote areas east of San Diego. A Christian preacher is droning away on the only station she can get, so she listens. He ends his show by asking for money to build a new retreat center, at which point Lily snorts, "Retreat for who? Sure thing. You tell 'em, preacher!"

As she drives, Lily surmises that her walkabout has been like a religious regimen. One day passing into the next, each nightfall a reminder that another day is gone. She believes that her journey, a freedom of leaf and pine, has been a primal nakedness and more worthy than any church service.

The hot southern California summer is in full swing, and Lily seeks the coolness of coastal ocean waters. She figures she can handle the crowds at the beach as long as she can swim out into the waves. Laughing loudly at herself, she says, "Homer, my walkabout is becoming a drive-about. What can I say?"

Her first stops are the towns of Coronado, Ocean Beach and Pacific Beach. At a small surf shop she purchases a beach towel, flip-flops and a blue flower bikini. In the full length mirror, she likes how her tan, fit body looks in the swimsuit. Usually uninterested in her appearance, she enjoys this momentary vision of herself.

As far down the beach as possible, Lily finds a fairly quiet place to lounge and swim. She breathes in the aroma of salt and fish and the pervasive citrus fragrance of sunscreen. The deep, fine-grained sand gets between Lily's toes, which feels weird after weeks of wearing boots. Enjoyable days pass with close-in, small-wave body surfing and sun-soaked catnaps. At night she sleeps in the back of Homer, which is big enough for a sleeping bag, clothes, and food. She parks Homer at assorted hotel parking lots where no one notices her or her overnight stays. Early some mornings, Lily sneaks in for a quick swim at a hotel pool. If asked, she's ready to say that she's a guest in room 114, but no one asks. There are outdoor showers and public toilets at most beaches. Life is easy.

Weekdays are not crowded, and Lily observes repeat locals at various spots. There's a hot looking young curly haired surfer dude, Declan, whom she enjoys chatting with. He's super sweet and has great beach recommendations. Lily ponders sleeping with him, but the real draw is his old dog named Jellie-belle, a big mutt of a gal. When Dex (as she calls him after a few meetings) goes surfing, he leaves Jellie with her. She and Jellie go for long beach walks and run around chasing each other at the shoreline. After a couple weeks of beach relaxation, reading, napping and taking long ocean swims, the hardest part of leaving is saying goodbye to Jellie.

• • •

Her next stop is an Encinitas campground, a barren group of parking spaces right on the cliffs between the Pacific Coast Highway and the beach. There are restrooms and wooden stairs that lead down to the ocean. Lily will have to share this bluff with RVs and highway noise, but the location is worth it. She sets up her tent on the pavement next to Homer and spends the first couple of days reading and looking out at the expansive Pacific. The sound of crashing waves and the scent of fresh salt air calm and exhilarate at the same time. It's a short drive to town, where she can support her espresso addiction and replenish her food stock. She finishes *Refuge*, one of the books she bought in Idyllwild. It was a hard read, as the author's mother is dying of cancer, a reminder of her own experience caring for her stepmother as she, too, died of cancer.

Edith arrives in a new white Volkswagen camper van and parks next to Lily's spot. After initial hellos, Edie, as she calls herself, opens a bottle of wine and grabs two long-stemmed glasses. She motions for Lily to sit in one of the two folding chairs perched on the bluff outside her camper. As she hands Lily a glass, she says she is taking a few days away from her husband. Her small body moves quickly as she talks. Her dark eyes scan the horizon as her hands flit from her long, brown, curly hair to the strap of her white tank top, to the edge of her cut-off denim shorts. Her large diamond wedding ring sparkles in the sun.

"We live in PB, Pacific Beach, me and my husband. I totally love him but he drives me crazy sometimes and I need to get away." Edie continues, "He wants to have a baby but I'm not ready, and I don't know if I ever will be."

Edie tells her the entire husband-and-wife baby discussion and Lily listens. At a lull in Edie's story, Lily pipes up, "Don't have a baby if you don't want one. I'm a product of that."

Turning to face her, Edie asks, "What do you mean?"

"My father had an affair with a young grad student, Gwen, who became pregnant. She was my birth mother, who died when I was five months old. Father took me to live with him and his wife, my stepmother. It was obvious they never loved me."

Edie pours more wine in their glasses. "That is very fucked up but you seem fine, even more than fine; you're cool."

"Thanks, but you don't know me and I really don't know what I am doing, what I want, or even who I am."

A colony of gray-and-white gulls fly overhead in classic V formation, wings spread wide, and both women turn their heads to watch silently. "You're still young," Edie says, "you'll figure it out. The best thing for you to do is just what you are doing, wandering the earth, getting out to sleep under the stars. I go camping to figure out my next step. My husband just bought me this camper, isn't it great?"

After a while, Edie says, "I think I could love a child, but I just don't want that responsibility, at least not now."

As they stare at another spectacular sunset, Edie invites Lily to hike the next day on a little-known path down to the beach called Fat Man's Misery. When they meet the next morning, Edie hands Lily one of two capsules of dehydrated psilocybin mushrooms. Each pops one in their mouth and they chug buckets of water.

The day is a scorcher. Brilliant blue skies radiate visual miracles and sunshine drills into Lily's entire body. Edie has taken mushrooms before but this is Lily's first trip, and it's heavy. Hiking down through the Fat Man's tightening sandstone cliffs, Lily feels like a bug squeezing through a tiny crack. The path is steep and very narrow and hours seem to pass as Lily's mind sifts through the dry earthen beige that envelops her. Edie, lost in her thoughts, seems to be breathing very loudly as she leads them down into what appears to be the center of the earth. Neither speaks until they emerge at the bottom of the Misery. Their feet hit sand as a thick blanket of fog settles along the coast.

"Can you see? I can barely see my own hands," Edie whispers to Lily.

Standing inches from where Lily sits, shifting her legs back and forth in the white sand, Edie waves her hands every which way in front of Lily's face. Minutes ease by, then Lily suddenly responds in a too-loud voice, "What? Did you say something?"

Edie starts giggling, long brown hair hiding her face. Lily reaches out to pull back Edie's hair and see her eyes. Looking directly at each other, they laugh hard, falling sideways, unable to stop their laughter. Who knows how much time escapes before they stand, holding onto each other for balance, both incoherent as tears of joy roll down their faces. Once upright, they gallop down the beach, hollering nonsensical sentences into the thick gray fog.

A mountainous-looking rock sticking up in the middle of the flat sand beckons them to climb to the top and perch there. The fog slowly dissipates and a robin's-egg-blue sky washes over as they sit, lost in their own silences. From out of the mist, a young man walking up the beach stops and stares up at them. He proceeds to remove his shirt, pants, and then his boxers, placing the clothes in a neat pile on the sand, then walks naked around their rock island three times. Slowly and deliberately, he dresses himself and walks leisurely down the beach. Stoned out of their minds, Lily and Edith think they have hallucinated the event, but in the course of time Lily whispers, "Did you see that?"

"You saw that too?"

They laugh so hard they need to crawl off the rock to pee in the sand. As they trudge back up the beach and climb up through the Misery, the heat of the day beats down on them. At the top of the cliff, Lily grabs another water bottle for each of them, then carefully drives Homer to their campground. After hugs, they go their separate ways to nap off the trip's residue. The next morning, as Edie gets ready to go back home, they promise to keep in touch. They never do.

Finding Blue

Close to the end of the third month of her walkabout adventure, Lily stops at a pay phone in San Clemente to call Norma. She has contacted Norma every week or two since leaving the San Gabriel Mountains. After a conversation about her latest campsite and Norma's garden, she stops at a taqueria for a veggie burrito and strolls to a nearby park to eat. The park is empty, as the day is foggy and a fine mist is in the air.

On her way back to Homer, she passes a dumpster at the edge of the sidewalk and hears whimpering from inside. Gingerly lifting the heavy metal lid, Lily can't believe it when she sees a small, bloody mass of black-and-white puppy fur, covered in pee. She takes off her sweatshirt and gently picks him up and wraps him inside. Puncture wounds and burn marks are on his upper back and neck. It appears that he has been tortured and thrown away to die.

BLUE

I don't remember the day Lily found me, but she told me that I looked three quarters dead. She said she carefully lifted me from the garbage and placed me gently in her sweatshirt. My tongue was hanging out like a dead dog's. Lily said I was the poorest look-ing thing she'd ever seen. I had no struggle left and didn't move as she carried me to her car and raced to the local animal shelter. The veterinarian told Lily I was about two months old, that I probably wouldn't make it, and that she would give me a euthanasia shot to put me down peacefully. But just as Lily was handing me over, I slid my tongue into my mouth and out again and gently licked her wrist.

When Lily tells the story to others, she leaves this next part out, but she tells me the whole story. In the sweetest whisper, Lily says, "Blue, I looked at where you licked my wrist and saw my scars un-der the wetness. That's when I knew you wanted to live. You just needed to know there could be love in this life." She always tells me this part with the little drops of water in her eyes.

Lily walked from the shelter with me wrapped in her bloody sweatshirt tied across her chest so I would be close to her heart. I was able to hear and feel her heartbeat, which she said helped me hold onto my life. We got back in the car and Lily said, "Little puppy, I think we need to go to Norma's house where I can better take care of you, and she will help me nurse you to good health."

A few hours later, as we pulled into Norma's driveway, Lily turned to me and said, "Your name is

Blue, and I want you to know: One's person's garbage is another person's treasure. You are now my treasure."

· · · · · · ·

Norma hears the phone ring. It's Lily, calling from a pay phone a couple hours south of Eagle Rock. Having spoken with her earlier, Norma is surprised, but when she hears that Lily found a sick puppy and is coming home, she is relieved and excited. She dashes to the vegetable garden to pluck cilantro, green onions, and chard. Back in the kitchen, she pulls out the large copper cooking pot, grabs cumin and curry spices from the drawer, and prepares a vegetable soup. In another pot she composes an egg porridge for the sick dog. While the food is simmering on her prized vintage Wedgewood stove, Norma mops the oak kitchen floor and goes back to the garden to cut roses to place around the house, including next to Lily's bed.

Lily was only eleven when Norma moved into the house next door, and over the years Norma has become like a mother to her. On one of Lily's first visits, Norma noticed scars on her wrist as she played on the ground with Norma's old hound dogs, Doolie and Dumplin'. Norma touched Lily's wrist and said gently, "It looks like you have some lonely markings right here. These little scars are to remind you to be strong. As you grow older, you will learn ways to find positive meaning in these sad markings."

Lily heard something in Norma's voice that made her feel cared for, something she had never heard in either of her parents' voices. Lily's parents rarely spoke to her or each other; their house was always oddly quiet.

When Norma's school-teaching day was over, she'd often ask Lily to walk with her and the dogs to the park. Passing house after house in their suburban neighborhood, Norma asked Lily all kinds of questions. Lily smiled and laughed as she told Norma stories about her backyard birds and the crazy tricks her squirrels did for peanuts. Norma listened intently and offered her hand for Lily to hold if she wanted. She always wanted. At the park, Doolie and Dumplin' would sit themselves down in the middle to watch all the other dogs run around. Lily asked why they didn't play.

"They enjoy being part of the dog activity, even though they're too old to play," Norma explained.

The following year, when Dumplin' died, and then Doolie a few months later, Lily thought her heart would break. Lily had never seen her stepmother or father show much emotion, much less cry. When Lily saw Norma cry, she cried too and held her hand. Lily cut out hearts and made cards for Norma every day to try to cheer her up.

• • •

Lily honks twice as she pulls in the driveway. Hurrying to the car, Norma hugs her and Lily tears up, overwhelmed. Carefully lifting Blue from the blanket, she hands him to Norma, who says, "Hello, little puppy, I'm glad you're here."

With words pouring out and tumbling over each other, Lily quickly tells Norma how she found the puppy. Walking through the house and into the spice-filled aroma of the sunny kitchen, Lily realizes she is hungry. She knows it will be a vegetable soup that Norma has made just for her.

Gently holding Blue, Norma says, "You know, honey, this puppy is very weak. He may not make it."

"Norma, he has to. I can't just let him die knowing only misery, it's too unfair!"

"I just want you to be prepared, Lily. We will do all we can."

At the stove, Norma picks up the pot of warm rice porridge with bits of scrambled egg and uses her finger to test the temperature.

Looking at Blue, who isn't moving at all, Lily says, "You try feeding him first, Norma, I don't know what to do."

Norma stirs the small pot, scoops a bit of the mixture into a rose-patterned bowl, then dips two fingers into the warm liquid cereal and slowly touches Blue's mouth with it. He doesn't respond. She and Lily watch and wait until they notice his little nose twitching, then his tongue slowly licks his porridge-covered lips. Norma does the same thing again and Blue once again slowly licks the porridge from his lips. Lily uses her fingers to do what Norma has done and Blue licks repeatedly until they think he has had enough. They don't want to overfeed him, as he is malnourished and his stomach is bloated. They continue to feed him every two hours, using an eyedropper to place water and the liquid medicine from the shelter veterinarian under his tongue.

After the first few days of constant care and hand feedings, Blue starts eating the porridge out of a bowl as Lily holds it. Sleeping most of the day, he is only awakened so they can feed him or put antibiotic cream on his sores. While Norma is at work, Lily curls up on the sofa with Blue, both cozily wrapped in a soft blanket while Lily reads the dog care books Norma checked out from the library.

BLUE

Lily rarely leaves my side as I get stronger. Sometimes I wake up to Lily's sleeping face right next to mine and I cuddle closer. When Lily leaves the house, Norma takes care of me. Her body, softer and more purposeful than Lily's, is like a warm blanket when her arms wrap around me. Her voice is deeper, smoother. It's like she sings her words. Smiling almost every time she looks my way, she'll laugh at any little thing I do. Now that I am getting stronger, she and Lily have taught me to pee outside and to sit before they put down my breakfast, lunch, or dinner bowl. They call it training when they teach me to walk on leash.

When Norma is home, between my lessons and playtime, she keeps herself busy doing dishes or laundry, vacuuming, working in the garden, talking on the phone, or moving things around. A few

weeks ago she brought home comfortable dog beds so I can lie down on my own pillowy place in the living room and in Lily's bedroom. My favorite place is the kitchen, where I eat my meals. Norma is a great cook and will ask me what spices I like and what I think about having vegetable crepes for dinner. I don't really get vegetable crepes—she or Lily feed me a stew made with kibble, canned meat, cooked vegetables and warm water—but I do like being talked to.

Lily tells me parts of my rescue story. She says it's important for me to know. "It took weeks, Blue, for you to start gaining strength, but once you did, you were unstoppable." Usually Lily ends the story with, "And look at you now, Blue, handsome is as handsome does, and buddy you are as handsome as a dog can be."

· · · · · · ·

Norma sings along to a Natalie Merchant song as she vacuums. It's Saturday, Norma's "Home Day." She coined the phrase when she moved into the first home she purchased for herself after her mother passed. That was nine years ago. Little did she know that the child next door would become like a daughter.

At forty, Norma loves teaching her fourth-grade elementary school students. Saturday mornings are spent on lesson plans and grading papers, then the rest of the weekend is hers to garden, clean, cook, and entertain friends. Her home is her sanctuary and each piece of furniture or object is a family heirloom or something she tactfully bargained for at a flea market.

The fuschia-painted entry hall has a Mexican pounded-tin mirror hung over a carved turquoise console table, both purchased with her mother after her father's death. During those sad days Norma began taking her mother to the flea market every Sunday after church, a ritual that lasted for years.

Pinning her dark, curly hair away from her face, Norma fluffs the bright orange-and-turquoise embroidered pillows and tucks them into the antique velvet sofa corners. She refolds the Mexican serape draped on the sofa arm, after which the saffron Turkish rug, her prize thrift store find, is vacuumed and the wooden coffee table dusted. Nearly a half century ago, her father carved this coffee table as a wedding present for her mother. Thinking of her parents, Norma kisses her own hand then touches the table. Bold paintings, family photos and odd treasures cover the walls. Plants grow in a variety of pots, each placed to catch the best light. Done with housekeeping, Norma happily grabs her book and goes outside to read in the patio garden.

When Lily Met Mac

Though quite content to be home with Norma, Lily is not thrilled about living back east of The Angels. It's not her terrain, it doesn't have enough open space or fresh air. Working part time as a barista, Lily is somewhat bored. She hankers for something more, maybe some male company, not to mention that good sex would be a nice addition to her now way-too-virginal lifestyle. Lily thinks she might call Big Mac.

She remembers the day she met Mac, before she left college, before her walkabout. Spring had arrived, a mix of cerulean skies and satin white clouds. Lounging on the grassy quad, Lily closed her eyes and let her thoughts drift for a few minutes. Absentmindedly, she pulled her hair to tighten her ponytail and cleaned her sunglasses with the hem of her long gypsy skirt. Glancing up, she noticed a guy sitting on a bench nearby, sloppily chomping on an extra-large MacDonald's hamburger. Bursting out laughing, she impulsively called out, "Hey, it sure looks like you're enjoying that!"

He responded, "Yes I am, ya want some?"

Lily replied, smiling, "No thanks Mr. Big Mac. I bet you don't know that you're eating parts of two hundred cows."

Like an uncontrolled magnet, the guy came to sit beside her on the lawn. Surprised by his movement, Lily was reminded of a big cat's fluid grace. Up close he didn't look catlike at all, more like a bear with shaggy brown hair, a large chest in a faded "Live free or die" t-shirt, and long, sturdy legs pouring out of baggy gray shorts. His smile and face seemed remarkably open and uncomplicated. Warm brown eyes, thick lashes and tattoos of vines and roses crawling up his right arm finished Lily's first impression of him.

The food conversation quickly led them to agreeing that they both disliked Lucky Charms, as neither found their luck changed when they ate it. They both liked chocolate. Lily laughed, "Who doesn't like chocolate? Maybe that discussion is of no import."

Mac responded, "Discussing things of no importance is important, don't you agree?"

A few days later, when they saw each across the lawn on their separate ways to class, Lily called out, "Hey, Big Mac, how ya doin'?"

Mac yelled back, "Wanna go to a movie? If so, meet me at the burger bench after class." Lily waved.

After his first encounter with Lily, Martin Michaelson had a bit of a crush. He immediately told his best friend, Tay, about his new "Big Mac" nickname. Since childhood, he and Tay had tried on cool names as often as they put on clothes. Martin's favorites for himself had been Monster Mart, Double M, and Madman; the last was the only one to stick with his buddies because it was the furthest from the truth.

Martin knew from an early age that his life would have something to do with moviemaking. He had always been a movie fanatic; growing up in Los Angeles, he eventually wanted a career with a studio. At eighteen he got a job working bottom-of-the-barrel movie construction, and when he finished college, he hoped to get his foot in the door as a set designer.

On their first date, Martin (aka Big Mac) took Lily to a foreign film. His first-date test with a new woman was always a foreign film. If she didn't want to read subtitles or didn't like the more artful movies, that would end the relationship before it started. Lily cried during the movie, and afterwards over a veggie dinner, she talked about the characters as if they had become new friends. Though Martin didn't like to think of it this way, Lily passed his dating test with flying colors.

At dinner they told each other a bit about themselves and their lives, something that Lily rarely did, but she felt comfortable with him. He knew how to listen, and when he asked questions, she felt that he wanted to know her answers. When she told him her father was a professor at their college, Occidental, Big Mac knew who he was. He had not taken any classes with him but was aware of her dad's reputation and said, "He is known to have his head in the clouds and his eyes on the young female grad students." Martin caught himself. "I'm sorry, Lily, that's not very nice of me to say. He's your dad."

"I don't care, I know his reputation," Lily responded casually. "I have never felt close to my father, and frankly he's not really in my life. A few years ago, after my stepmother died, he sold our house and started living with his latest girlfriend. I moved in with my neighbor, Norma."

Big Mac told Lily he was close with his parents and rolled up his shirt sleeve to show Lily the top of his rose vine tattoo engraved with the word "Mom" and a small heart.

"You're really lucky," Lily responded, "I don't know what that would be like."

• • •

Flashing back to that first encounter and their early dates, Lily calls Mac and leaves him a "Hi, I'm back in town, do you want to hang out?" message. She is pleasantly surprised when he calls back the next day, and they agree to get together over the weekend. It's been almost five months since she last saw him. Lily wonders if this is just a booty call for her, or maybe a callback booty call for him, she has no idea.

Opening the door to Mac's knock, she notices a large scar crossing his left eyebrow and blurts, "What happened to you?"

Chuckling, Mac answers, "Well, hi to you too, Lily."

"Sorry, I know my manners suck."

Mac responds, "Yes they do, and I already know that about you."

Smiling, trying not to be obvious as he scopes her out, Mac is once again intrigued. She looks tanned, almost rugged. He feels a bit in awe of her as he says, "I'm glad to see you! I want to hear all about your travels, but since you asked first, I'll tell you what happened to my face . . . at least the short version."

"Be my guest," Lily replies as she walks into the living room.

"Okay, so I have to say I was really drunk. No excuse, but I'm using it."

"Please go on."

"My buddies and I were hanging out at this seedy bar downtown, just letting off steam. Truthfully we were being assholes and acting like a bunch of spoiled college kids, ya know, obnoxious. We were walking out of the bar when I tripped over this biker dude's boot and said rather loudly, "What the fuck, move your goddamn foot.""

Picturing the scene, she likes that Mac doesn't hide behind an image, that he accepts who he is, flaws and all.

Mac continues, "The next minute we're in a fight, me and him, then my buddies and his. These guys were tough, well versed in their street fighting skills, so we got the shit kicked out of us. The brawl moved from the bar onto the sidewalk when the boot guy pulled out a switchblade and took a swipe at my face. I yelled to my buddies, 'RUN!' We pushed them off us and ran like crazy as they stood back and laughed. The boot guy yelled, 'Run home to your mommies, you little fucking babies, and don't come back.'"

Mac looks at Lily. "I'm an idiot sometimes. My friends rushed me to the hospital and I got eighteen stitches. Maybe you should call me Scarface."

"No thanks, I'll stick with Big Mac. I'm sorry that happened to you, that sounds really stupid and scary. I'm glad you're okay." Lily gets up from the sofa. "There's someone I want you to meet."

BLUE

A couple of months after we move into Norma's house, I meet Big Mac. Lily dated him a few times before she found me. Big Mac likes me a lot. Now that I am about four months old, healthy and much bigger, Lily, Mac, and I take short hikes around the canyons and parks scattered around The Angels. Mac is a great ball thrower and will hurl that ball so far up in the sky I can barely see it. I run like crazy and when I catch it in my mouth, he and Lily cheer and clap. Even though I am young, I have to say that I am really good at ball sports.

Not to brag too much, but as we are on the topic of my skills, I am really good at a lot of things: I can sit and lie down and stay, I walk very well on the leash, and Lily says I am an excellent student. Everyone says I am very smart, everyone meaning Lily, Norma, and Big Mac. The thing I do the very best is eating. Norma tells me that I am an Olympic gold medal eater. I don't quite understand because I have never eaten any gold medals, but I know it's a good thing because Norma laughs when she says it, and feeds me a bit more.

• • • • • • •

Nesting

A few years older than Lily, Mac has graduated college and is working construction in the film industry. He is often away on various jobs, but when he's in town he joins Lily and Norma for dinner. A group effort, Mac usually brings groceries and a bottle of wine, and helps with the cooking. These are fun dinners with plenty of snacking, spice discussions and happy laughter.

The house is small and as time goes on, Lily notices that Norma retires to her bedroom after they wash dishes and finish the kitchen clean-up. Lily mentions to Mac that Norma may want more private time. The next time Mac is over, Lily asks Norma about the little cottage behind her house.

"You know it's filled with storage, why do you ask?"

Lily looks at Mac, who explains, "Norma, we'd like to fix it up as a permanent living space for Blue and

Lily, and I would pay you rent to stay there when I am in town. It's just an idea. We understand if…"

Before he can finish, Norma interrupts, winks at Lily and Mac and says, "I think it's a great idea. When will you start?"

Relieved to have help going through the storage items that have been on her to-do list for years, Norma asks Lily if there's anything she'd like to use. Lily picks out a small kitchen table and chairs and an old floral chintz-covered settee.

"That was my mother's favorite, I am so glad you like it," Norma says.

"Oh Norma, are you sure?"

"Please, Lily, I have been feeling guilty all these years keeping it in storage. I know she would want you to have it. What about these stainless pots and pans? And look, this box has mugs, plates and glasses."

Lily puts these boxes into her "yes" pile, along with a brightly colored rag rug she finds tucked in a cor-ner. Norma hands Lily a few ceramic pots to take to the garden, which later they will plant with arugula, cilantro and Thai basil. The rest of the stored items will go in the garage sale planned for the next weekend. Lily and Norma mark prices on everything and Norma bakes cookies to hand out at the sale.

Smiling, she says to Lily, "I believe in sweet incen-tives."

To Norma's delight, almost everything sells. With the money she purchases a hand-carved Mexican bench she has been eyeing in a local thrift store to place in the patio.

Mac builds an upstairs loft in the cottage and creates a spare, industrial-style kitchen underneath it. He covers one whole wall with used barn wood and installs old windows that Lily finds at a salvage warehouse. Windows open up the space to view the small backyard. In the bathroom, Mac replaces a generic sink with an old porcelain trough sink they find on the street. Lily paints the bedroom a soft lavender and one kitchen wall a rich cobalt blue.

Succulents, shrubs, and a small plum tree are growing in the postage-stamp backyard, and Lily adds bird-friendly penstemon, salvia and lavender perennials to the fragrant roses that border the patio between the main house and cottage. The last bit of their makeover is a birdseed platform and a hummingbird sweet water feeder.

Once it is complete, Blue saunters through the back cottage door across the patio and into Norma's kitchen. He can't believe these two houses are his! Each time he enters Norma's house he acts as though he is on a great adventure, sniffing the kitchen cabinets, wondering if there might be a snack or two for him. If he finds Norma talking on the phone or correcting class papers at her desk, he lies at her feet; if she is cleaning house, he follows her from room to room.

50

Life has settled down east of The Angels. When Mac isn't working, he spends most of his time with Lily and Blue, hiking, hitting the movies, and going to various restaurants and bars. He invites Lily when he goes to see his family, but she makes excuses not to go. Sometimes she hangs out with Tay and his other friends but she hasn't met his parents yet.

At her barista job, Lily makes a few friends but mostly comes home after her shift to walk Blue. One of their habitual destinations, the Lady of the Lake stands elegant and powerful overlooking Echo Park. The simple mile walk around the lake ends with the art deco sculpture, a totem Lily touches each time before leaving the park.

At home in the garden, she can spend hours training the squirrels to eat peanuts from her hand. It's not an easy task, and she realizes what a patient child she must have been. A squirrel she named Jasper is catching on to the peanut game. Sitting on his hind legs to get a peanut or two in his mouth, he runs to find just the right hiding place, sometimes in a flowerpot or the conch shell tucked into a corner of the garden, or under a throw pillow on the farthest chaise. He then hurries back for another peanut and his search for a hiding spot starts all over again.

One day Norma gets a call from Lily's father, asking if Lily still lives with her. He wants Lily to call him. Norma gets his number and goes to the cottage to tell Lily. A long discussion follows about what he may want, as he has not been in contact with Lily since she left Occidental more than a year ago. Lily knows he would only contact her because he wants something. Deciding not to involve Big Mac in her decision, as he has no idea what she went through as a child, she waits a few days then asks Norma to sit with her as she calls.

"Hello, why did you call me?"

Father responds, "Well, that's not a nice way to start a conversation with your father. I called you three days ago. What took you so long to call me back?"

Lily takes a deep breath and instead of throwing the phone across the room, she again asks why he called.

Her father blurts, "You are so selfish! I'm in the hospital. I had a heart attack and need to rest for a while, and I need some help."

"What kind of help?" Lily is close to tears and doing her best to not scream at him. Struggling to keep her voice calm and low, she asks, "Where's your girlfriend?"

Father explains that she is traveling for a couple of weeks and he needs someone to take care of him. Lily tells him she will call him back and quickly hangs up.

"What should I do, Norma? He wants me to take care of him."

"Of course he does, Lily, but you don't have to if you don't want to. He has plenty of money to hire someone. Remember you are no longer a child, and the decision is yours."

Lily calls him back and says she has no time to help him, and that he should hire a caregiver until he can take care of himself. She asks how long he will be in the hospital. Her father says he will be released the next day and loudly tells Lily, in his most professorial tone, that she is just like her mother, selfish to the core.

"Thank you for your input. I hope you feel better soon." As soon as she gets off the phone, she bursts out crying.

Norma grabs Lily and hugs her, practically shouting, "He is a total asshole!"

Lily laughs through her tears, as Norma never talks that way. As it plays out, Father is back teaching within a few days; his heart attack was not a serious one. Lily is left wondering which "selfish mother" her father was referring to, her birth mother Gwen or her stepmother.

With the aid of long talks with Norma, Lily recovers from her father's phone call, and for the better part of another year Norma, Mac and Lily enjoy their lives and each other's company. Then, seemingly for no reason, as if an alarm bell has gone off inside her, Lily's internal roller coaster slams into their tranquil lives.

East of The Angels has never really been Lily's kind of place. She loves Norma's house and cottage, but once she walks out the front door she's hit by the suburban city, all of which holds nothing for her. Suffocated by too many buildings and people, she's like a caged animal pacing back and forth, longing for fresh air and open skies. Lily can't seem to relax; she retreats into an inner silence where her mood is dark, her actions edgy. She quits her job and spends her time sleeping, reading, and taking long hikes with Blue. Instead of drinking or smoking pot a few nights a week, she partakes every day and every night and is loaded pretty much 24/7.

Noticing Lily's behavior change the last few weeks, Norma asks if everything is all right, to which Lily responds in an irritated voice, "Norma, everything is fine." Which, of course, means it isn't.

Mac can tell something is bothering Lily, so he brings her flowers and little presents and takes her out for special dinners. He finds an exotic animal and wild-life sanctuary in nearby Sylmar called Wildlife Waysta-tion, a 160-acre rescue sanctuary for animals who have been injured or abused. Lions, zebras, llamas, bears, ti-gers, foxes, peacocks, and other birds and animals from mismanaged zoos and circuses as well as chimpanzees from medical biological laboratories, all live out their lives with care. He hopes this will jump-start a happier mood, but after their visit, Lily is more depressed than ever. Though the animals are well cared for now, the stories of their past lives devastate her and she silently cries the entire way home. Walking into their cottage, she grabs a bottle of wine and holes up with Blue in their bedroom with the door locked.

An old, cavernous feeling is taking hold of Lily; her body feels like a thin, brittle surface filling with a darkening sadness. No lightness or joy seems able to enter, no matter what anyone does for her or says to her. As much as she is loved by Norma and Mac, she can't feel it. She is drowning and the only way to stay afloat is to get high.

One day, Norma comes home from work to find that Mac has made dinner, set an elaborate table on the patio, and has candles burning. *Oh, no,* Norma thinks, *I hope I'm wrong.*

At the end of dinner, Martin takes Lily's hand and asks, "Will you marry me?"

Lily tears up. "I need to think about this. I don't know, but thank you." She kisses him on the cheek. "I will sleep on it."

Norma quietly says goodnight to each of them and goes into her house.

Mac accepts Lily's need to think it through, but the next day, when he and Norma return home from work, Lily and Blue are gone. A note lies on the kitchen counter: *I have to go. I love you both.*

She just up and left, like a bird flying right out the door.

Runaway

As she and Blue head east in Homer, Lily says aloud, "What just happened? Shit, why did Mac ask me that, what is wrong with him? He couldn't possibly love me! Marry me? I don't get it. Blue, what *is* love, anyway? I know I love *you*, but you're a dog, you're easy to love."

It's midmorning when Lily notices a silence stretched from one end of her to the other, like an old, vacant house. She tries to be excited that she's on the road again. Turning on the radio, she flicks through stations until she finds something she likes. With the car windows down, she lets the open highway breeze surround her and sings along.

Late that afternoon, Lily calls Norma to say she's sorry she had to leave. Norma's worried; she tells Lily she loves her and asks her to take care of Blue and herself. Lily says she will and bursts out crying when she hangs up.

Big Mac can't believe that Lily left without talking to him. Besides feeling like his heart has been crushed, he feels like an idiot and talks Norma's ear off.

Norma listens for a while, then says, "Marty, I know you're hurting. You may not understand this, but Lily is lost; she is not heartbroken or bewildered, she is *lost*. She doesn't know the *there* that is there. I'm sorry to say this to you, but she was smart to run. She knows somewhere in herself that she's not ready to love someone when she barely loves herself."

Holding his hand, Norma continues, "Martin, I think you know yourself, you probably always have. That doesn't mean you don't have hard times, or don't question yourself. And I'm sure you feel just awful sometimes, like now. But some people need to find themselves. Lily's one of those, and she's looking, she's looking hard, but that doesn't mean much until she finds who she is."

Mac looks down, wavering between pain and anger. He knows that Norma is right, that Lily is a mess, he is starting to understand that. "I get it, asking her to marry me was a stupid move on my part. I could tell she was depressed and I just didn't want to lose her. But she knows me, we could have talked this through."

"*You* may have been able to talk with *her*, Marty, but she isn't capable of doing that now. She ran away, not only from you and me but also from herself. One day I hope she will realize that and come home, home to where she is loved. When I was young, my *abuelita* told me to trust the people I love, to trust them and accept what they need to do for themselves. Marty, try to trust Lily. Right now she has her own road to travel and you have yours. You know what that is, so go do it."

After walking around in a daze for two weeks, Mac receives a letter from Lily saying that she and Blue are in Flagstaff, staying at a campground. She writes that she's sorry, that she really cares for him and probably loves him, but she's not ready to settle down and be with one person. For the first time in his life Mac has no idea how he feels; he just knows he needs to stay busy with work. He moves out of the cottage and into an apartment in Studio City.

BLUE

Lily and I are in Homer again. She put my food and bowls in the back of the car along with bags of clothes, a tent, and a sleeping bag. On our long drive to the Southwest, Lily tells me she said goodbye to Norma and Big Mac for me. She says she feels badly but she can't marry Big Mac now, she had to leave. Water keeps falling from her eyes. I lick her hand because I love her.

Lily says, "Thank you Blue, I love you too."

I nod my head, then look out the window while Homer stays on the road and Lily turns the steering wheel. The air is warm and when Lily rolls down the windows, my ears flap in the breeze. I am ready for anything as long as I am by Lily's side.

• • • • • • •

Their first overnight in Joshua Tree is dry, extremely hot, and smells like pungent incense. At five pm it's 112 degrees and the rocky sand burns Blue's paws when he gets out of the car. Lily pours bottled water to quickly cool his feet and has him hop back in Homer. They drive around awhile until they find a shady spot to pitch their tent.

Even in the shade the heat is debilitating. A couple of weeks ago Lily bought a new two-person tent and it's the first time she has set it up. Hot and irritable, she finally gets it put together, takes out the weed she's brought, and lights up.

By the fourth hit, Lily tells Blue, "It's like this, my little prince. Smoking cannabis relieves the stress. Well, maybe it just hides it, but that's okay too." Looking at their tent, she asks Blue, "How do you like the name Alice? I think we should name the tent Alice, like Alice in Wonderland." Blue looks blankly at her. "Well, my little love, you look a little noncommittal about the name, but maybe you're too hot to think about names right now. Let's keep it for a while and see if it fits."

Surrounded by cholla, Joshua trees, saguaro, yucca, various lizards, hot baked rocks and a dry wind, Lily soaks a towel with water and lays it on Blue's head to cool him. Lifting Homer's tailgate, she removes a guitar case and book and sits next to Blue. Trying to re-member songs she taught herself to play years ago, she takes time tuning the strings and looks over the chords in the guitar book. Mother gave her this guitar before she died. It was surprising as Lily never heard her play nor seen the guitar, which had been buried in the back of a closet.

When she gave it to Lily, Mother said, "You have a good voice, I've heard you singing in the backyard. I used to play guitar long before you were born. I was even in a band." She hesitated and sighed. "But that was a lifetime ago. If you want to learn to play, I think you will be good at it."

That was the nicest thing Mother ever said to Lily. When she died and Father sold the house, Lily bought a few how-to-play-guitar books and started teaching herself. Once she learned a few songs, Norma would sing along with her. Though she practiced on and off for years, Lily never got serious about playing. While living with Mac she stopped playing, she doesn't know why. She tries a few simple chords, directing her tentatively sung words at Blue, who perks his ears.

The next morning the ground is still too hot for Blue's tender paws, so they pack up and continue driving southeast. Bypassing Phoenix, Homer heads toward Sedona and the red rock country, reaching Pine Flat Campground just before dark. It's almost full, but Lily finds a small camp spot on the bank of the west fork of Oak Creek. Red canyon walls are visible though the canopy of ponderosa pine and the campfire ring has leftover wood. There is good swimming along the river, so she and Blue hightail it to the creek for a quick bath and a bit of water play before darkness blankets the canyon. Alice is set up and made comfy with the help of the lit campfire and a flashlight.

Breathing in the scent of pine, Lily sighs happily and puts half of her peanut butter sandwich in Blue's bowl of kibble. Pulling out her maps, she explores the locations of power vortexes in the area. Usually skeptical about all kinds of energy healing, Lily is somewhat interested here, as it is earth energy. Growing up in Los Angeles with Reiki healers, Scientologists, and all kinds of shamans and gurus on every corner, Lily has learned to sift through what she considers bullshit.

The temperature is cool and crisp. Lily revels in the high desert air, the beauty of Cathedral Rock, and the rusty red soil contrasting the bright azurite sky. She and Blue find the vortex near Bell Rock and sit, allowing the swirling earth energy to enter them.

With her arm around Blue, Lily asks, "My dear earthling creature, do you feel anything? I'm not too sure if I do, but it does seem there is a vibe here." Not waiting for his answer, she continues, "Do you think it's the iron oxide in the earth, or that Native Americans have lived here since 4000 BC?"

Blue shakes his head because sometimes that's what he does.

After vortex sitting, they go into town, where Lily sees a man and woman playing flute and guitar on the sidewalk. They're not that good, but she puts a dollar bill in their open guitar case and asks, "Nice music, do you make much money playing on the street?"

They nod and say they do okay. It's only noon and she notices they already have about twenty dollars in tips.

Back at the campsite, Lily takes out her guitar. As she strums the strings, Blue howls at certain notes. Maybe it's the vortex they sat on or maybe it's copycat understanding, but Lily has a brainstorm: She can make traveling money by singing and playing guitar while Blue does his tricks and acts his usual goofy self.

On a walk around the campsite late that afternoon, Lily sees magpies hopping around scavenging for tasty food morsels left by careless campers. They fly and swoop from tree to tree, cawing loudly at each other as if showing off, and Lily finds herself laughing. The well-dressed desert cousins of crow, raven and jay, magpies have shiny black feathers and long tails that show off hints of blue and green iridescence next to their snowy white shoulders and bellies. Inspired by these corvids' intelligence, energy and antics, Lily names her guitar Magpie.

That night in front of the campfire, she focuses on her fingers as she plays the chords to a new song, "The Rose" by Bette Midler. Blue is her number one fan. Lily sings, "Some say love, it is a river that drowns the tender reed," and he gets up to strut his various walks, including his backward shuffle. Lily thinks his shuffle looks like Michael Jackson's moonwalk.

At the end, when she sings, "I say love it is a flower and you its only seed," Blue lets loose with a mournful howl. Lily looks at him with admiration. "Well, my prince, you are one talented dog!"

Arriving in Flagstaff the next week, Lily gives it a try. Along with "The Rose," she has practiced a few songs: "Blowin' in the Wind" by Bob Dylan, "Both Sides Now" by Joni Mitchell, and the old classic, "Summertime." She loves the version by Billy Stewart from 1965 that Big Mac turned her onto, but Lily's voice can't go there, so she does her own simple folk rendition. She buys Blue a turquoise bandana neckerchief to wear, and as soon as Lily ties it around Blue's neck, he prances and wiggles his butt. Lily chuckles and says, "You are going to be good at this, my little showboat."

Lily chooses a place to sit on one of the main streets and unlatches her guitar case, leaving it open for tips. She tunes up, looks at Blue, and starts playing. On the street a couple people stop for a minute, but walk on without leaving anything. Knowing she needs to sing, Lily is scared and shy and instead has Blue do tricks, including an acrobatic tree flip where he runs up the trunk of a tree and does a backflip to land on all fours. Passersby stop and clap, providing an opportunity for Lily to tell Blue to moonwalk as she picks up her guitar and sings,

> I've looked at clouds from both sides now,
> from up and down and still somehow
> it's clouds' illusions I recall.
> I really don't know clouds at all.

Money lands in her guitar case with thank yous and head nods from strangers. While Blue is busy being admired by dog lovers in the small crowd, Lily, flustered by the attention, whispers, "Thank you, thank you," and packs up the guitar. She calls Blue to come and they head back to Homer.

Late that night, holding the flashlight, Lily counts sixteen dollars onto her sleeping bag. She is floored; hugging Blue, she tells him, "This is gonna work, buddy! It looks like I'm gonna be your backup band and banker."

Flagstaff is the kind of small town Lily likes, built in the midst of quiet natural beauty, and the people she meets are chill. They stay at Canyon Vista Campground and venture out to explore local trails. The patchwork of meadows next to ponderosa pine and aspen forests and along the paths are tranquil, nothing like the drama of the red rock canyons near Sedona. The joy and freedom that Lily initially felt on her walkabout a few years ago are gone; she hikes now because that is what she does. She still loves to hear the birds sing, watch the deer and elk forage for food in the morning, and splash her legs as she walks through canyon rivers or swampy lakes. She fills time with motion, nothing more, nothing less.

Leaving Blue in Alice at night, she goes to the local bars and comes back late, stoned and drunk, usually with some new guy she doesn't care about. In the mornings after the guy leaves, Lily sleeps most of the day and Blue naps beside her. When Lily wakes she's in a down mood, so she rolls a joint, heats water for tea, and starts her day late in the afternoon.

One day after buying a few things at Safeway, she and Blue stop to watch a woman haphazardly maneuvering a shopping cart across the street. The woman drops cardboard boxes and clothing in the busy intersection. She and her dog run back and forth a few times, retrieving then dropping items, again and again.

Her young shepherd seems to be enjoying this catch game, though the woman looks frantic.

Lily asks, "Are you okay, can I help you?"

As the woman opens her mouth, Lily sees a piano of teeth with every other key missing, the existing teeth brown and rotting. Though not old, this woman looks done in; meth has grabbed her and thrown her by the wayside. The woman responds, "I'm kinda hungry."

Lily takes a twenty from her wallet and hands it to the woman. "It's going to be cold and rainy tonight. Do you have enough to keep yourself and your dog warm?"

The woman takes the bill and peers closely at it. Lifting her eyes, she looks straight at Lily and states, "Some people are kind."

The next morning Lily says to Blue, "We're out of here. It's gotten a little depressing around this town." Blue looks up and wags his tail. "You know what, my little prince? You're lucky to be a dog, humans can be so unhappy. Well, not all humans; Big Mac and Norma seem happy, but Mother and Father definitely weren't. Maybe I got it from them, or maybe I inherited unhappiness from Gwen." Sighing, Lily touches Blue's soft front paw. "Sorry, buddy, I have no answers." Lily kisses Blue on his furrowed forehead and says, "We'll be all right. I'll make you food and then we'll pack up Alice and head out."

Blue hears "food" and wags his tail.

Misty Roses

They arrive in Taos late the next afternoon. The dry, thin, high desert air leaves little overlay for creature spirits to veil themselves, and a mystical ambiance invades everything. As a chatty local tells Lily when she purchases food supplies, "All spirits float freely on the mesa."

This ancient sculpted earth is somehow known to Lily, and the essence of sky and open space permeates her being. Feeling clear and lucid, she confides to Blue, "Ya know, buddy, I'm not too sure where I belong, but I feel more at home here than I have felt anywhere. It's like I understand the air here, like it's a place I've lived before." Blue looks at Lily as he always does, with devotion and love. Over the next weeks, these two explore the desert mesas and mountain forests, the lost and the found interweaving their lives.

BLUE

Lily and I scour and sniff every trail and river we can find near Taos. By nighttime my body is very tired. Many evenings after dinner, Lily leaves me to sleep in the tent while she and Homer go off somewhere. When she comes back she smells of booze and smoke. Some nights she doesn't come back at all. When that happens, I worry.

· · · · · · ·

Sitting in a dark corner of a Taos bar, drinking a beer by herself, Lily looks out the window at the night sky. A sad quietness wraps around her like a soft velvet cloak.

It's a Saturday night and Ethan Tanaka has come into town for a rare night out. The moment he walks into the bar he sees her, out of nowhere a childhood song comes to his mind, an old Tim Hardin song his dad used to sing:

> You look to me like misty roses, too soft to
> touch, but too lovely to leave alone...
> You look to me like love forever, too good
> to last, but too lovely not to try.

Every time his dad sang, he would tell Ethan, "I love his music. Tim Hardin was only thirty-nine when he died, way too young."

Ethan asks Lily if he can join her.

"If you want," she she replies. It's such a simple answer and not out of the ordinary. It isn't the words she says but how she says them, so quietly, as if she's speaking her own secret language. Ethan understands right then that he wants to know her. It is not like Lily is beautiful, as she is a bit stocky and plain with long, tangled hair, but she has an intrigue, he thinks, and maybe a kind of hidden wisdom. One glance into her deep-set hazel eyes and Ethan sees old pain held there, as well as a wildness bordering on otherworldly. Her eyes remind him of a goat's eyes, the one he found out on the mesa a few years ago, wrapped in barbed wire. The goat stared into Ethan's eyes as he slowly untangled him and carried him to his truck to bring home. The goat was like an old soul and lived well cared for on Ethan's ranch for a couple years, until he died of old age.

After their first meeting, Ethan looks for Lily at this bar or that. She doesn't seem to care one way or the other if she sees him, but a few encounters later, when he asks her to a local gallery show and out to dinner, she agrees to go.

During dessert, Lily inquires, "You're kind of a dreamer, aren't you?"

"I guess I am. I think you are too," Ethan responds.

"Definitely, I know I am, which may be the only thing I know about myself. Back to you: Your initials are ET, like extraterrestrial. Has anyone ever called you that?"

"You mean ET? No, but I get where you're going, and it's okay. 'Ethan' is kind of proper, but I think it fits me."

"It does, and so does ET."

After a few more dates, ET asks if she wants to drive out of town in his pickup. She agrees, and they get stoned and make love out on the mesa. Looking up at the stars balancing in the chilled night air, Ethan is held captive as Lily dreamily points to the edge of the sky.

"Look, Orion is just coming into view. Do you know his story?" She whispers, "There are lots of versions of this myth, but my favorite is the one where Orion was a celebrated hunter who boasted how he would kill all the animals of the earth. The earth goddess Gaia didn't like his boastfulness or his desire to kill animals. She became so angry that she banished him and his two hunting dogs, Canis Major and Canis Minor, to the sky, where they could chase the animals but never catch or harm them."

Lily points again, "See there? Those three stars on Orion's belt are sometimes called the Three Sisters. They have many names and there are many stories about them as well. I like the one where the three sisters, who represent family, bloodline, and belonging, were cursed to carry all the sorrows of the world." Lily is quiet for a moment, then says, "The youngest carries all the world's sighs; the middle, the world's tears; and the eldest carries all the darkness of people's souls."

Lily's voice fades away and she rests in ET's arms. She feels comfortable in his embrace. It's not love but it's more than convenience. Other than that, Lily doesn't know or question her feelings. Ethan has little idea of who Lily is, but thinks that over time he will learn more about her. He trusts her in a way he hasn't trusted many of the local women. Thirteen years older than Lily, he observes that she is young, that she smokes too much dope and drinks often, but he thinks they somehow fit. Two dreamy nature nerds in love with poetry and books.

An artist in a small town, Ethan meets a lot of women. He is handsome with a slight build, broad shoulders and a naturally toned body. He wears his thick, black hair pulled back in a long braid and dresses casually, but no matter what he wears, he looks elegant. Though he is an introvert and fairly quiet, he has become well known in the community for his artful modern ceramic vessels and water fountains. The women he usually meets think he is someone he is not. They don't understand that he leads a simple, almost spartan lifestyle and doesn't want more than that.

His best friend Javier told him once, "It's that male artist thing. Women are attracted to creative men . . . until they get to know them." Laughing, he said, "I totally love you as my lifelong best friend, but as a boyfriend and partner, I wouldn't recommend you!"

Ethan agrees. He thinks of himself as fairly selfish; his craft, his garden and his animals come first. He's particular about his use of time and goes into town as little as possible. When Ethan meets Lily and sees her quiet ways, that she doesn't put on airs or pretend she's someone she isn't, he is drawn to her. He brings Lily to his house a couple of times and they spend the night together. Ethan notices that she likes Cleo the Cat, the goats and chickens, and that she seems to enjoy being alone as much as he does. ET worries that Lily might leave town, so he asks her to move in.

Lily answers casually, "Sure, why not?"

BLUE

One day, as I am lying in the sun outside our tent, I see a man in a broad-brim hat walk up to our campsite. He and Lily hug and he says hi to me, pats my head, and helps us pack all our belongings in Homer. Then Lily, Homer, and I follow his beige pickup to a house and stay a very long time. His name is Ethan Tanaka, Lily calls him ET.

The first thing I notice at his house is that there are lots of animals. ET has four goats, five chickens and a cat. He says he used to have six chickens but a coyote ate one of them. I get excited when I hear this—I want to eat chickens too!—but Lily reads my mind. She says, "Blue, I know what you're thinking and I understand how you feel, but you are *not* allowed to eat these chickens. We are now part of their family, so you must protect them." She gives me that look of hers that makes me go all googly-eyed, then says, "You are such a good boy." From then on, I make sure the chickens don't get eaten by me or anyone else.

ET's house, which he calls a "ranchette," is in Tesuque, just outside Santa Fe. I love lying in the sun on the warm, dry dirt and watching the cotton trees sway in the breeze. Even in the cold of winter, ET's house is cozy and warm. After bounding through snowdrifts, I go inside and sleep in front of the large stone fireplace. Cleo the Cat sometimes leans her furry body against mine and she even sleeps on my back, which feels weird but also kind of good. We are friends. Then there are the goats, who like to eat as much as I do but they eat crazy things like flowers, shrubs and wood. I'm not gonna eat that stuff. Well, sometimes I will eat grass if my tummy is upset or chew on a stick just for fun, but that is totally different.

Living with ET feels safe. I have plenty of good food and ET is kind, though not as fun as Big Mac with the ball playing and running around stuff. I often follow ET as he does his work around the ranch or in his studio. He gently pets me on my head and behind my ears. He says, "You are a smart dog, Blue, I am glad you are here helping me with this fountain."

I don't really help him with his work, but I like that he says that. He and Lily read a lot of books, mostly after dinner, while I lie on the sofa with them or on my pillow by the fire.

. . . .

Ranch Life

In the mornings, Lily and Blue let the goats and chickens out of their pens and feed them breakfasts of fruit, grains and vegetables. She lets them wander the farm as she uses the pitchfork to clean up the old hay and put out fresh for the animals. Before leaving the barn, she and Blue lie down in the fresh mound of hay. Ethan wanders in and lies with them. Looking up from their straw bed, Lily and ET lazily chat while Blue rolls around in the fragrant dry grasses.

Today when they leave the barn, two magpies glide in. Lily gets them food as well, and as time goes on, the magpies come find her when she whistles. Lily remembers childhood mornings when she whistled for her squirrels. She thinks she was meant for farm life, even if her earliest farm was two squirrels with home-made cardboard-box homes.

Lily asks ET if the goats have names. Chuckling, he confides that he named his goats after his favorite Southwest writers. He has never told anyone other than his friend Javier, as he doesn't want people to think he's too eccentric. Reaching for his hand, Lily says, "I name everything, including my car and tent. This part of you is probably one of the reasons I like you."

As ET introduces her to each goat by name, Lily recognizes each goat's distinct personality. "This is Simon, he's the largest and friendliest. He is named after Simon Ortiz, a Native American poet and fiction writer. Barbara here is the oldest, named after Barbara Kingsolver. She is a bit quirky and reserved, but very kind. She'll wait her turn for treats when others push their way in. Frank is an old crusty goat and can be quite bossy. He's named after Frank Waters, who wrote *The Man Who Killed The Deer*. Frank lived in Taos years ago." ET ends his introductions with his youngest goat, Linda. "I named her after Linda Hogan. This may sound a bit crazy, but I think she is the poet of the group. Everyone loves her and it seems she holds some special power just by being here."

Having read Linda Hogan's poetry in college, Lily says, "Why not? This little goat has very wise eyes."

As the chickens do not have individual names, Lily decides to take that on. She finds that hens, too, have their own distinct behaviors and personalities. They can be quite elegant like Jacqueline, or worried about everything like Gladys. Lily is surprised at how smart and companionable they can be. Annette likes to sit in her lap, and Pearl is bonding with Blue and will nestle right beside him when he sleeps in the sun. And then there is Lucy, short for Lucinda, who is always first: first to eat, first to the garden, and first to run up to cackle hello.

Ethan makes a mental note to have date nights, trips to town, and hiking adventures with Lily. When he becomes totally absorbed with his work and stays in his studio day and night, his usual excuse, "All artists are like this," won't work with Lily. He wants to be a better partner than he has been in the past.

In his mind, Ethan checks off Lily relationship "easy things." Both of them are avid readers and enjoy nights together with their books by the fire; both are animal people, enjoy gardening, and are homebodies. When ET enters the house, he sees Lily perusing the bookshelves in the living room and adds "good sex" to his list. At this point, he isn't interested in investigating the red flags waving in the corner of his mind. Joining Lily by the bookshelves, he asks, "What are you looking for?"

On his well-organized shelves, Lily sees the wide range of his reading tastes. There are rows of artists' books, architectural and construction manuals, historical biographies, and all kinds of fiction and adventure novels. "You have a wonderful library. I think I will start my reading with the authors of the goats' namesakes. Who do you think I should read first?"

ET suggests, "Start with Frank, he's really interesting, then I would suggest Barbara."

"Thanks." She reads book jackets and chooses a Barbara Kingsolver novel.

Lily's days are spent with the animals and reading, and a few days a week she and Blue wander local trails, sometimes bringing Magpie, her guitar, to play and sing. She hasn't played in front of ET yet, but maybe eventually. She tests recipes with the local chili peppers and various types of corn and squash. No matter her activity, Lily partakes in pot smoking or wine sipping or both. Cleo has taken to following Lily and Blue everywhere. Ethan feels a bit neglected, as Cleo is his best animal buddy, but this is exactly the life he has always wanted.

Quilts

"Can I use this?" Lily asks ET. Looking for boots in the hall closet, she has found an old sewing machine.

"Whoa, I haven't seen that in years, of course you can use it. I learned to sew in elementary school and made all kinds of hippie-trippy shoulder bags in high school."

ET runs into their bedroom, digs in the closet and pulls out a brown and maroon corduroy book bag to show Lily. "This is the last one I have." Looking at the bag, he laughs, "I guess I was always an entrepreneur. I sold dozens of these to friends in high school. Not the most creative, but it was cool to see people walk around with something I made."

Lily looks at ET and says, "Wow, you were so brave. I would have been too insecure to ever make something I thought might sell."

"It was probably Waldorf, the school I went to. We all made stuff that was mediocre but we got lots of praise for it." ET grabs the sewing machine from the floor. "Let me oil it and get it working for you."

When Lily was eleven, Norma taught her to hand-stitch a skirt hem, along with sewing simple things like pillowcases and dish towels. Thinking back to one of the first days she went to Norma's house, Lily recalls touching the long magenta velvet drapes in Norma's living room and wrapping herself in them. They felt soft and silken, like diving into a warm bath of creamy raspberries. Later that week Norma gave Lily a magenta velvet pillowcase she made from leftover material. Lily slept on that pillowcase every night for years. Norma also baked chocolate chip cookies just for her. Lily loved watching Norma take milk out of the refrigerator and pour it in an old silver pitcher, then serve her an ice-cold, tall glass of milk to drink with her cookies. She thinks now that Norma wanted her to know she was a most important guest, that she was special. Lily puts her hand to her heart and whispers, "Thank you, Norma."

Lying on the sofa, smoking a pot ciggie and dreaming of her past as cornbread bakes in the oven and vegetable soup simmers on the stove, Lily thinks about Mother and Father's house. The stark, modern, beige interior lacked warmth or any lived-in feeling. It looked normal from the outside, as a gardener came every other week, but once inside, the paintings on the walls were a beige design to match the sofa, the floors were covered in beige carpeting, and the coffee and dining tables were glass and chrome. It was colorless and cold. Lily has no memory of sitting with Mother or Father in the living room or at the dining table. They had no idea how to love or raise a child: They never ate meals together, played board games, or shared their stories of the day. Lily feels a heavy, silent pressure inside and falls asleep. Jolted awake by the smell of burning cornbread, she jumps up and runs into the kitchen. It is too far gone to save, but nothing goes to waste, the goats and chickens will enjoy their share of the burned cornbread. Luckily the soup is still fine, so Lily makes a new batch of cornbread for the humans.

· · ·

Lily is on a roll. After reminiscing about her lifeless childhood home, she decides to sew something to add more color to ET's house. First she improves her sewing skills by creating dog and cat toys from a couple of old shirts. The toys are odd-shaped and silly cloth creatures. Blue tosses his around and up in the air to catch, while Cleo takes hers and hides it in the garden. Confident enough with her sewing, Lily takes a trip to the fabric store.

Thinking of Norma's house, she purchases a rich turquoise velvet to make two throw pillows for the sofa. ET, mostly involved in his own work and unaware of many things going on around him, is impressed with Lily's creative focus and compliments her.

Next, Lily decides to make a quilt for their bed. Having spent too much money on new fabric, she goes to the Goodwill where she finds a long, rectangular piece of embroidered Guatemalan fabric for three dollars. There are rich red and hot pink roses vining up the center and the background is tightly woven denim-blue cotton. At the bottom of a material scrap pile, she discovers four yards of bluebirds in a flower garden. She likes the cotton fabric and the price of two dollars.

Intense days of cutting and sewing follow, and Lily's creation becomes a lush quilt of rose vines in a garden filled with wild birds and surrounded by shades of blue night sky. She sews pillow covers to match the blues of the sky. Lily spreads the finished product over the bed and calls ET to see it.

Leaving his studio for a short break, he looks closely at the sewing and design. "This is beautiful, Lily, very artistic and well sewn. You are extremely talented."

His praise is too much for Lily so she bonks him on the head with a pillow, which starts a pillow fight and ends with them racing around the house like two little kids, throwing any pillow they can find at each other. Tumbling on the sofa, tired and laughing, they end up holding hands as they lounge around, talking about this and that. ET asks if Lily might like to make another quilt and pillows for the guest room.

Happy to oblige, Lily starts a farm-inspired quilt. She cuts various plain and printed fabrics in the shapes of chickens, goats and two magpies, along with a Cleo-looking cat and a Blue-looking dog. Next she cuts out tomato and chili pepper plants, marijuana plants and cornstalks. Weeks go by as Lily hand-appliqués animals and plants on a background of high desert colors sewn into a farm-style landscape, including a barn and fences with snowcapped mountains and aspen trees in the background. A large sun shines bright yellow and clouds drift in a periwinkle sky. When she is done with the quilt, Lily sews corn-colored velvet pillowcases to match. It's a masterpiece.

Ethan can't stop talking about her intricate design. He suggests they drive up to Taos for drinks and dinner to celebrate her arduous task and brilliant artistry.

Lily likes the sound of all this. "Good idea, let's have a night on the town, but don't start thinking of any more sewing projects, I'm done."

Shocked by Lily's "done" statement, ET feels an emotional blip for the moment but lets it go. He has dedicated his career and life to his art and has no understanding of what being "done" means.

BLUE

Every few weeks, Lily takes me on what she calls a walkabout. We pack Homer with Alice, our tent, the sleeping bag, a flashlight, my food and water bowls, Lily's food, and other stuff and drive to someplace Lily wants to go. It's cold and gets dark early. We take a short hike though big trees and sometimes there's snow on the ground. I love when there's a pile of snow to jump into. When I do that, Lily laughs. Otherwise she is pretty quiet unless she brings Magpie, then we sing together by our camp-

fire. We set up our sleeping bag in Alice and Lily reads while I nap. Then we eat peanut butter sandwiches and take another longer nap until the air is light again. It's very quiet unless the wind is howling outside. I would rather be home next to the fire, but Lily needs me.

· · · · · · ·

Target Practice

ET worries about Lily on her overnight excursions. The bears are hibernating, but there are mountain lions and weirdos out there. Blue is good protection but not for everything, so ET gives Lily one of his handguns. Lily has never shot a gun, so they decide to make a scarecrow to shoot at.

That night, as she sits on the rose vine quilt covering the bed, Lily asks ET to pull out some clothes to help decide what the scarecrow should wear. When he brings a gray suit from his closet, Lily exclaims, "Where did you get that?"

"My mom, of course. I grew up in Los Alamos. It is a strange mix of people there, from mad scientists wearing baggy corduroys and ink-stained pocket pen holders to very conservative suit types. My mom is a suit type."

"That's pretty obvious, but not your dad?"

"No, my dad does his own thing. He listens to a lot of rock and roll, golfs and mountain bikes, and loves square dancing."

"Really, square dancing?"

"Yup, and as a scientist he reads and questions everything. Being a Japanese American living in New Mexico, he has a mistrust of some humans and felt he needed a gun for protection. As far as I know, he only used it for target practice. Living out here on the ranch, I feel the same way."

"That makes sense," Lily agrees. "Let's go with this gray suit and your white-and-blue pinstripe dress shirt, that red striped tie, and what the fuck do you have a John Deere baseball cap for? We're using that for sure."

ET smiles at this choice of scarecrow attire. As they dress the straw body, ET asks, "Is he well endowed?"

"No, that may be one of his problems," laughs Lily.

"You're harsh!" he jokes.

She winks at him. "You started it! He's a businessman gone bad, what do you think he's done?"

"Hmmm, a firing squad is rather harsh punishment for simple graft, so he did that and committed several murders to hide his thievery."

Lily adds, "And he hurt and killed animals.

As shooting practice starts, Ethan tells Lily exactly what his dad taught him. "A gun is for protection, and if you are not going to use it, don't take it. If you do have to use it, shoot three times. Always shoot three times. Shoot to kill or you will be killed. Keep the gun loaded and near you at all times."

Lily has fun shooting at the suited scarecrow and becomes a good shot. When ET questions her, she says she understands the rules, but he's not too sure.

Corn and Marijuana

Spring arrives and the garden becomes Lily's sanctuary. Lettuces, green onions, carrots, and zucchini are planted and will eventually tumble over the raised beds. Rows of corn and sunflower starts intersperse with marijuana plants, and wine barrel tubs of tomatoes and herbs scatter here and there. By summer Lily is baking berry pies, carrot cakes and fresh cornbreads.

As far as the marijuana, ET smokes occasionally, but Lily chain-smokes her hand-rolled joints and is into an array of beer, wine, and other alcohol.

The well-loved and cared for garden is in full glorious bloom, but Ethan and Lily's relationship is not. They have become like siblings bickering over little things, and are no longer lovers. Neither can pinpoint when things started to turn.

Most of their earlier care and thoughtfulness for each other is now directed toward the garden, the animals, and anything but each other. Lily is far from present and loaded most of the time, and Ethan escapes to his studio. Sometimes friends come over, ET's friends, as Lily has not tried nor felt the need to make any of her own. She likes his friends and they seem to like her.

Tonight's dinner is potluck, and being a good host, Ethan welcomes everyone. At dinner they tell stories, discuss politics, and berate or rave about music and movies. The evening sparkles with conversation and laughter. But after the goodbyes, and after Lily and ET clean up the dishes and kitchen, they go their separate ways. Lily heads to the bedroom to read and smoke more dope, and ET wanders the ranch, ending up in his studio until late into the morning.

Visiting from their home in Los Alamos, Ethan's parents, Becky and Howard, arrive Sunday for their bimonthly brunch. Tension runs high when Becky walks into the kitchen to find dishes in the sink. Lily has baked cornbread and cinnamon buns, and has the chicken eggs ready to make an omelet, but all Becky can see are dirty pots and pans, and that Lily is already drinking wine. Unpacking the sunflowers, orange juice and a ham, Becky does not want to accept that Ethan and Lily are vegetarians and have a garden full of sunflowers. Lily reminds herself that it's the thought that counts and thanks Becky. Ethan walks in the kitchen and hugs his mom.

"What shirt is that you're wearing?" Becky asks. "It's so old."

"I like this old shirt, and how are you?"

Ethan loves his parents and accepts that his mother is extremely talented at finding fault. Howard comes into the kitchen singing along to an album he just put on the record player, a Crosby, Stills and Nash song from the '70s, "Wooden Ships." Ethan joins in as they carry the food to the table. Howard gives Lily and Ethan hugs as he continues singing, and at the chorus he grabs Becky by the hand and dances her around until she too is smiling and singing along.

> Wooden ships on the water, very free,
> easy, you know the way it's supposed to be.

Ethan smiles, as he knows his parents love each other, and Lily holds his hand for a moment. At lunch Howard pours himself a glass of wine and makes a toast about how delicious everything is. He tries to lighten the mood as Becky quizzes Lily: "Are you going back to school? What kind of job do you want? Maybe you could become a chef if you went to school, would you like that?"

It's all Lily can do to remain seated at the table. Minute by minute, she is shutting down.

Ethan takes her hand under the table and says, "Mom, stop please, it's too much."

At the same time, Howard says, "Becky!"

ET's mom does not like that Lily is thirteen years Ethan's junior, that she has no job, that she drinks too much. She thinks Lily doesn't love Ethan enough. Sometimes mothers know best, but Becky's attitude makes things worse and the stress is palpable. When his parents have gone, Lily and ET unload on each other, arguing for the rest of the day. By dark, Lily is so wasted that he has to help her to bed.

As the summer heat bakes into the dull, dry desert, Lily becomes more dissatisfied. It is clear that ET and Lily still care for each other, but they no longer pretend they can be a couple.

When Norma comes to visit the last week of August, she sees that Lily is lethargic, depressed, and in a downhill spiral. Lily tries to hide how she feels, but Norma digs in. "So what's going on Lily, do you want to talk about anything?"

"Not really, Norma." Lily seems to be done with this line of conversation, but as Norma continues to look directly at her, she blurts, "Okay, I'm not happy, so what? It's not a big deal."

"It *is* a big deal, Lily, and I'm worried about you. Do you know what your unhappiness is about?"

"No, not really. I just feel shitty, and then I become a shitty friend, and I don't want to do anything or talk with anyone. ET has tried and I appreciate that, but it really makes no difference to me. I'm being selfish, I know that. I don't want to feel sorry for myself, but I don't seem to be able to feel any different than I do."

"Maybe your body is out of balance, that can happen. Do you want to see a doctor or therapist?"

"I don't think so. I want to figure this out for myself."

"Are you sure?"

Dramatically sighing, Lily starts to walk away. "Yes, Norma, I'm sure. Just let me be."

Norma reaches out and grabs Lily's hand and holds it gently for a moment. "No, Lily, I won't let you be. You are too important to me, do you know that?"

Lily wants to pull her hand away and run out of the room, but she whispers, "Yes."

Norma remains silent for a moment, then says, "I want to say something to you. Will you listen?"

"Okay."

"After my father died, my mother was devastated, understandably, and went through a deep depression. She used to call it 'locked in', as in being locked inside yourself. When I tried to help her feel better, she said, 'You can't help me. I am in a prison of my own making, even God can't help me now. I don't know the way out, I'm sad and tired and I feel nothing good. So honey, if you want to help, I need a hug, and then maybe I'll need a push.'

"For my mother to feel that way was really scary for me. I didn't know if she would ever come out of it. But I gave her a big hug and then something came over me and I gave her a big push! I almost knocked her over, and we both started laughing so hard we ended up crying. Every time I saw her after that, which was almost every day, I would hug her and then give her a push, not as big a push as the first time, but we would laugh." Norma stops for a second, remembering. "Life is not easy, Lily. Sometimes you have to trust that you will feel better with time, and allow the hugs and the pushes."

Lily asks, "Did your mom eventually feel happy?"

"Yes, she did. I don't know if it was exactly feeling happy, maybe it was more like feeling connected to her life. But maybe that is what happiness is, being deeply connected to your life and the life around you. She went through the time she needed, then one day she said, 'I'm good,' and started living her life again. She loved her life right up to the end, which was different than how she had lived with my dad. She had loved him so much, but I think she blossomed into her very own person after that."

Norma smiles at Lily and says, "Are you ready? Cause I'm going to hug you and then I'm gonna give you a big push. The rest will be up to you."

Before Norma leaves, she, Lily, ET and Blue hike the trail out to the Rio Grande Gorge. An electric-blue sky intensifies the flatness of the land as mountains stand sentinel, boundaries to the mesa's limitless expanse. Distant bird calls and the crunch of their shoes pounding the dry rocky earth are the only sounds to break the high desert silence. Partway to the gorge, Lily stops to gaze at shifting cumulous clouds, half-crystal white domes with flat, plum-gray bottoms rolling, piling and bumping rudely into each other. Topping the mountains to the east, dark imposing clouds lie suspended, waiting for an unknown wind to push them into the valley. Lily stretches her arms wide to embrace this magnificence of place. Continuing down the trail, she spots a large dead beetle whose body has become an open cafeteria for an army of red ants. Something twists inside her and she hurries to catch up with the others.

Norma has prepared a simple picnic of cream cheese, tomato and arugula sandwiches, and lemon cupcakes. ET brought extra bottles of water, knowing Norma is not used to the altitude or the dry air. Silently they eat, sitting at the edge of this precipice as the liquid-brown Rio Grande snakes and twists at the bottom of the ancient, jagged cliffs. Their thoughts are lost to the thousands of years that echo through this deep chocolate canyon.

Before Norma leaves, she entreats Lily to bring Blue and come home for a while. Lily says she isn't ready.

Come early October, Lily informs Ethan she is leaving. He doesn't want to say it out loud but he is relieved. Together they pack up her and Blue's belongings.

The last thing Lily says as she hugs ET goodbye: "You're a good person, ET. I am so sorry. I will miss you and Cleo and the ranch."

BLUE

When we leave the goats, the chickens, ET, and one of my best friends forever, Cleo the Cat, we travel up

through northern New Mexico through Navajo Nation lands, where we stop and camp in Monument Valley. The wind blows dry dirt and sand at us as we walk the trails. Lily loves the huge sandstone buttes that tower over the flat, red desert floor. They have silly names like Mittens, Eye of the Sun and Ear of the Wind. At night the temperatures drop to chilly cold, so I crawl in Lily's sleeping bag where her body keeps me snuggly warm.

After driving all day and camping at a small, almost empty campground, we stop in Zion, where Lily hikes by herself for much of the day. I sleep in Homer, under the shade of a huge tree outside the park. "Sorry, Blue, I know this isn't fair, but most dogs are not as well behaved as you are, so dogs are not allowed in national parks."

Hours later I am awakened when Lily joins me in the car and tells me about the Narrows, a deep slice in the mountains where she walked through a river. Smiling, she tells me about the climb to a lip of a rock called Angels Landing, where she felt like she was standing at the edge of heaven. I listen politely but I'm distracted by thoughts of food, burgers in particular. Lily lets me out to pee, and I get all excited when she says, "Let's get something to eat."

We stop at a drive-in, and as though she can read my mind, Lily orders two burgers for me and a vanilla milkshake and fries for herself. At a park we sit at a picnic table and Lily hands me small bites of burger while she sucks her drink through a straw. Delicious.

Heading west the next day, we land in Las Vegas, where Lily tries our street singing and entertaining again. It's been a long time, because when we lived with ET we didn't do any of our street work. Lily tells me we may be a bit rusty, but not to worry. She has improved her playing on Magpie and I am, of course, very skilled with my tricks. We set up on the main drag. Lily puts a new turquoise bandana around my neck, opens Magpie's carrying case, and drops a few dollars in to get people to start tipping. She turns to me. "Okay Blue, let's do our thing."

Over three days, we shift our location to different streets; everywhere it's crowded with tourists clapping, some singing along to the songs. Lily tells me, "Blue, you have done a great job."

We sleep in Homer one night in a hotel parking lot, then rent a hotel room the second night. Lily says we've made enough money, and since Vegas is kind of creeping her out, it's time to leave. She says she saw a burger joint on the way out of town. I like the sound of that.

At Joshua Tree, the weather is much cooler than our first time there. We stay many nights and take short, dusty day hikes where we have fun scrambling over small rock outcroppings. I have to be careful of the prickles when I lift my leg to pee on some cactuses, they are dangerous. Lily is in a good mood. She plays Magpie at night by the fire and we sleep late into the day. When she wakes, she cuddles with me, massages my ears and scratches my belly. I love Lily.

We head to Palm Springs and work the streets again. Lily says she is enjoying this. My moonwalk needs work, so I practice in front of the customers and they clap and pet me. We make good money the first day, but Lily gets super drunk that night and loses it all, so we stay until one day she says, "Blue, pack your bags, it's time to move on."

This time of year there are few tourists at Lake Arrowhead and Big Bear. It's cold but there's no snow, and we hike trails and camp in Alice under the stars. One night Lily looks at me and says, "You know, Blue, I thought camping and hiking would help me feel better, but to tell you the truth, I don't. I'm starting to think it's not *where* I am but *who* I am, and it sucks. I'm tired. Let's head back to Norma's, okay? We can be there in a day."

Okay? You bet it's okay, I totally miss Norma and her kitchen, and all the comfy resting places at her house, and our cottage.

When we get home, Norma cries and throws her arms around Lily in a big hug and then hugs me big time too. I'm smiling like crazy and my tail is going wild. Lily tells Norma how tired she is, and Norma says the bed in the cottage is ready for us. That first night I stay and sleep on Norma's bed. She tells me, "Blue, I'm happy you're both home, but I am worried about Lily."

I try to tell her that I'm worried too. I hope we will stay at Norma's forever, but it doesn't turn out that way.

• • • • • • •

Back East of The Angels

The divisions of fall, winter, spring and summer have little to do with the weather in the City of Angels, as it's pretty much sunny all year, but Lily is in the midst of her own arctic winter. Retreating to the little cottage, she stays in bed smoking pot and reading most of the day. Blue sleeps beside her on the bed until Norma comes home from teaching, when he jogs over to her house for love and special food. She has taken over making his dinner, as well as food for Lily.

Purple and blue salvias intermingle with pink, purple, and red roses in the garden patio between Norma's house and the cottage. Norma makes sure the garden is watered and the bird feeders and squirrel peanut baskets are full. Usually when Lily is home, that's her job. She used to enjoy lying on the outdoor chaise watching these little creatures eat their fill, but these days she has no interest.

Hoping for a festive Thanksgiving, Norma asks if Lily wants to see Big Mac or ask him to join them.

"No, he's seeing someone, and he's leaving soon for a set design job in North Carolina. Anyway, I'm not in the mood." Being in the cottage again, Lily's mind wandered to thoughts of Big Mac, but they don't last long. She's glad that he's not available, or she would probably see him and it would make things worse.

Norma cancels her Thanksgiving plans to spend it with Lily. She makes a simple dinner and tells Lily how thankful she is to have her and Blue in her life. Lily tries to say something but any kind words are hidden in her dark mood.

A couple of weeks after Thanksgiving, Norma decides she will celebrate Lily's twenty-fourth birthday with a new pair of hiking boots and socks, along with ice cream and a cake with twenty-four candles. With tears in her eyes as she blows out the little flames, Lily makes a silent wish. Blue enjoys licking the remains from Norma's and Lily's plates.

Raised Catholic and still somewhat of a believer, Christmas is important to Norma. Carrying a box of ornaments from the closet to the sofa, she sits and says, "Lily, this holiday is not about you; this is for the memory of my parents, so please be helpful and try to enjoy the holiday season for me."

Every year, Norma carefully unwraps her grand-mother's pottery nativity scene and wall crucifix, and her mother and father's indoor statue of the Virgin Mary holding Christ as a baby. There is a permanent outdoor statue of the Virgin of Guadalupe in the midst of the patio rose garden. Her father said a prayer to her every day, and during the holidays Norma says prayers and lights candles at her base. Lily recognizes this image of the Virgin as the patron saint of Santa Fe.

The variety and number of trees at the Christmas tree lot is overwhelming. Lily, Blue, and Norma quickly walk past the blue, pink, and white flocked trees, then linger in the natural green area of tall, wide, short, and spindly trees. Blue enjoys lifting his leg on a few lower branches until Lily notices and tells him to stop. After some discussion, they settle on two small trees, one for Norma's living room, which they put on a table by the fireplace, and one for the inner patio, placed so it can be seen from both houses. They spend the evening unwrapping ornaments and colored lights to hang on both trees and around the house.

Norma plans a potluck Christmas Eve party and invites her friends, most of them teachers. They bring food and drinks and gather in the kitchen, talking loudly and sharing stories. Andrew brings a variety of Christmas music CDs, traditional carols and Motown Christmas songs, and for Blue a CD of dogs barking holi-day songs. When Blue hears it, he goes wild, howling along with the first song. With everyone laughing and watching him, he is in his element. He begins with his moonwalk then shows off any other dance step he can. Everyone claps and cheers and does their own versions of moonwalking and crazy dog dancing. Lily laughs for the first time in months.

Norma grabs Lily's hand, beckoning her to join, which she does for just one dance. Andrew and Miriam smile secretly at Norma, as she has confided her worries to them. It feels weird to Lily to share Norma's attention, as it's obvious that she is adored by her friends. Norma has always been *her* special person, and though she doesn't want to admit it, she feels a bit jealous.

New Year's slips by with Lily in a pot stupor. Aware of how often she is stoned, Norma knows something is stuck in Lily's heart. She wonders if she should make Lily see a therapist but leaves it for Lily to decide. One night as they are taking down Christmas lights and ornaments, Norma asks, "Lily, do you want to see your father?"

"No. Did he call again, is something wrong with him?"

"No, I just thought I'd ask, in case you did want to see him." Trying to sound nonchalant, Norma asks, "Do you want to talk with a therapist I know, or maybe one I don't know?"

Again, Lily demurs.

Norma can't stop. "I'm worried about you. Is there anything I can do? You know you can talk to me about anything. You do know that, Lily, right?"

Lily stops what she is doing and stands still, pointedly staring at Norma. "Yes Norma, I know that. And yes, I know I am a wounded creature, and if I want help I will tell you. I'm not stupid. This is my problem and I will figure it out or I won't. I'm not ready for any-one to help me."

Later that week, chopping vegetables for dinner, Norma tells Lily the story of when she first saw her as a little girl, in her backyard talking to the squirrels.

"When I moved into this house, I could see you playing in your backyard from my kitchen window. Whether you were sitting by yourself reading or feeding and talking to the squirrels, you looked like one of the loneliest children I'd ever seen. I've taught hundreds of children with all kinds of families and difficulties, and I worried about you. But I could see that you, more than most, had amazing gifts to share."

Lily continues chopping as Norma continues, "Your empathy and patience were remarkable. Your stubbornness and sense of adventure, as well as your compassion, were evident even then. Lily, you know stubbornness can be a gift when we're young, but it can become a burden as we get older, that's something for you to think about. Compassion is forever, and you have an abundance of that. I thought then that your gifts would see you through, that it would just take time, and I still believe that."

"Is that true?" Lily asks, sitting on the kitchen stool with tears in her eyes.

"Without question," Norma replies.

Lily and Blue stay until late January. Norma hates to see Lily leave again and offers to keep Blue while she goes where she wants.

Lily says, "I need him with me." She is rested, but emotionally not healthy. Norma asks her to keep in touch. Lily doesn't answer. Norma reminds herself that Blue has a locator chip, so if he gets lost, he can be found. But Lily doesn't have an identity chip. She could become lost forever.

BLUE

As Lily packs Homer with Alice and all our camping gear, her clothes, Magpie, my water and food bowls and lots of food, I know we are leaving Norma's. I lick Norma's face and lean my body against her legs. I don't want to go, but Lily needs me. I have to make sure she is safe.

Driving to Santa Cruz, Lily tells me she knows a girl from college who lives there, but we don't end up visiting her. I relax as Homer moves along the road and Lily turns the wheel.

As it turns out, we stay in Santa Cruz about a year and a half. I love the beaches, the forests and all along the river. The first year is pretty exciting, while we explore the whole area and perfect our street act. But as time goes on, I become worried. Lily always has a can of beer or a bottle of something in her hand, she smokes more weed than ever before, and sometimes she swallows small pills of various colors. She smells different and sometimes forgets to feed me.

People hang out around our tent, and most of them don't pay any attention to me. They get loud and boisterous and then they just leave. Lily leaves me alone in Homer or in Alice many nights. I'm not feeling well, and when I'm hungry or thirsty I visit other people who camp along the river. Some are nice, and feed me chips or cookies and a few times, hot dogs, but sometimes people throw rocks or yell at me. Once I got fed these squiggly puffy orange things and everyone laughed because of how I had to chew them, as they were very spicy. Later that day, when Lily saw the orange on my lips and around my mouth, she scolded me, saying that what I had eaten wasn't food. From my perspective, if I can eat it, it's food. Lily doesn't notice that I scratch and chew my skin all the time trying to catch the little bugs that crawl over my belly, under my legs, and around my tail.

Not that everything is bad. When Lily isn't sleeping all day, she and I hike the redwood trails behind Santa Cruz and through the open spaces of the Pogonip. We play frisbee at the beach, and if the weather is warm enough, we swim. Best of all is when she buys me a hamburger or feeds me plenty of kibble. And no matter what, a few days a week Lily cleans us up a bit and we do our moneymaking act on the streets. Some days I am amazing, doing backflips and moonwalking, but other days we bomb, mostly because Lily is too drunk or stoned to play and sing. One day we fell asleep right there on the sidewalk and a policeman woke us and yelled at us to move on.

. . . .

Sinkhole

It's not like anything suddenly happens, it's more like a fog that slowly drifts in and eventually there's no blue sky left. Lily loses track of time. Well, really she loses track of everything, like a ball thrown for Blue that has not yet been retrieved. At some point during their time in Santa Cruz, Lily succumbs to the sinkhole of human depression. She starts hanging out with those who spend their days along the San Lorenzo River, a transient society of the homeless, addicted, forgotten, and unloved.

Lily wakes up again in a morning-after haze. She has puked all over the floor of her tent but is too tired to clean it up. With Blue's sad eyes staring at her, she falls back to sleep. Something has been turned off in her, or maybe it's just lying buried. She rarely thinks of Norma, ET or Big Mac. She's having nightmares; the creepiest one is being locked in a dark box, and all she can see are her fingers scraping at the wood above her.

Trapped in her world of denial, she has forgotten about the local squirrels and crows she once fed and talked to. The first months in Santa Cruz, these wild creatures became her friends. As her behavior slips and slides downhill, she forgets almost everything she loves about life. She no longer sees the pink edges of the clouds at sunset, the iridescence in the splash of a wave, or the gentle gray early morning mist. She has become just another loser, living outside, not seeing what is right in front of her.

In the late afternoon, Lily unzips the tent flap and tells Blue to go potty. She crawls out to take a pee, bracing herself on one of the poles of her well-worn tent. Noticing the tossed-away food wrappers and empty water and vodka bottles at her feet, she thinks, *Fuck it* and crawls back to sleep, forgetting all about Blue, who is looking for food at nearby tents.

Lily wakes as the sun is setting. The sky is sprinkled with pink and purple cotton-candy clouds, but all Lily can do is grab a warm beer from the corner of the tent and light a joint. She takes a dirty yellow towel and wipes up the puke on the tent floor that has been festering and stinking all day. After changing her clothes and wiping her face with a wet washcloth, she crawls from the tent to look for Blue.

Blue is nowhere to be found but Lily runs into Mikey and Jewel, the local river power couple. Mikey and Jewel have been together for years and are the hub for recreational drugs. Mikey will give you the shirt off his back—but don't ask for any free heroin, he doesn't go that far, that's his main moneymaker. Jewel is on a roll, telling Lily how she misses her daughter and that she is planning to go to rehab so she can get her back from Social Services. Lily has heard this before and listens sadly as Jewel's dark brown eyes tear up and she runs long fingers through her short, dark hair. Jewel dream-talks about a future with her little girl while Mikey looks lovingly at her, saying nothing.

Wearing his trademark black leather pants and sleeveless white t-shirt, Mikey is the river godfather, kind and judicial, and as Lily has heard, sometimes brutal. In his early forties, he is short and grizzled. His ink-illustrated arms are always in motion and his eyes constantly scan some personal visual perimeter, a habit from years of watching out for cops. Jewel, tall and thin and looking like the model she was once was, is ethereal, thoughtful, and quiet. Like tranquil river water, Jewel moves and talks slowly. She tells Lily about a party up-river, offers her "E", and they wander upstream.

Empty bottles of beer, bourbon, and vodka are scattered everywhere, and a few people are drumming as others dance or throw themselves every which way. Thirty or so people are in various stages of oblivion, and Lily feels the Ecstasy coming on strong. She chugs from a vodka bottle and wanders the crowd. Seeing Josh, a guy she lived with for a while last winter, she greets him, "Hey Raccoon, how are you?"

"What did you call me?" Josh yells in her face.

Drawing the half-empty Smirnoff bottle to her lips for a quick swig, Lily places her hand on his shoulder.

"You're so cute, you look like a raccoon."

Josh snarls, "You're drunk. I'm glad you moved out."

Slurring her words, "I sure am. And you may be lookin' all raccooney and cute, but you're nasty. You know raccoons are assholes." Lily straightens her t-shirt and plants her dirt-covered feet solidly enough to stand. "And by the way, asshole, you're a spoiled brat who can't even be nice to my dog."

Josh looks away. "Fuck you, Lily."

Lily chimes in, "Yeah, we did that already." Catching herself before falling down, Lily staggers off to find Jewel, who will have weed.

• • •

Last winter had been a particularly wet and stormy one. Sleeping in the back of Homer, Lily loved the sound of the heavy rain on the metal roof. At some party one night, Lily met Josh and ended up sleeping with him at his apartment. After hanging out a few more times, she and Blue moved in.

Josh was gone most of every day, working at a computer company over the hill. In trade for the accommodations, Lily cooked meals and cleaned his apartment, which consisted mostly of sidewalk finds: an old, stained, brown leather sofa, round laminate wood table with four mismatched chairs, and a bed. At first Lily wondered how he owned a state-of-the-art TV and high-end stereo equipment, always had great dope and lots of alcohol, and could afford to go to concerts and restaurants. She soon learned that Josh had recently graduated from University of California Santa Cruz and his parents were from the wealthy enclave of Palo Alto. He played poor to his friends while his parents paid his rent and gave him whatever he wanted. Lily quickly lost any romantic interest she might have had. She doesn't like posers. As soon as the rains abated, she and Blue left to again stay in Homer and Alice.

Two days after the river party, Lily wakes up in her tent. She can't remember where she has been or what drugs she has taken, other than the "E" she took with Mikey and Jewel. Her clothes are torn and she wonders how she got so many bruises on her arms and legs. Vaguely, she remembers laughing and falling down a dirt cliff with a tall, thin, wispy blond-haired guy. Taking off her t-shirt and ripped jeans, she is glad to see her underpants and bra are still intact. *I would remember if I had sex*, she thinks. She recalls a big bonfire in a clearing in the redwoods, and lots of people and bottles and blunts passing freely from hand to mouth.

The stink in her tent is nauseating from the puke of a few days ago. With a water bottle and a somewhat clean towel, she is washing her face, armpits, hands, and feet when she hears someone yelling her name. Quickly pulling on clean pants and a shirt, she crawls from the tent onto the hard-packed soil. The sun beats down on her as she slowly stands up. Through bleary eyes she sees a heavily tattooed, beautiful young woman coming toward her.

"Are you Lily Harmon?"

"Yes."

"My name is Jonnie and I work at the City Animal Shelter. Do you have a dog named Blue?"

"Yes, he's not here, I was going to go look for him."

"He's been picked up as a stray and is at the shelter again. I know you bailed him out a few times this past year, but this time he is covered in sores. He is extremely thin and constantly lunges at the kennel door. He has been deemed unadoptable and is scheduled to be euthanized tomorrow or the next day."

Lily can't stop staring at this young woman, who looks like a mix of Halle Berry and Jennifer Lopez but with the full-on, no-bullshit attitude of k.d. lang. Wearing bad-ass Doc Marten lace-ups, high socks, ripped jean shorts and a man's sleeveless plaid shirt, she is practically bald and has tattoos covering her arms and parts of her legs. Her gait is very distinct and Lily wonders what animal this woman reminds her of, but her thoughts are interrupted.

"You know the shelter is not a hotel for animals. Your dog has been living in a cyclone-fenced cage with loud barking around him all day and night. It's a stressful place for any dog to be, especially a sensitive dog like yours. He's losing it. I have taken care of him in the past and I know how smart and sweet he is. He looks like shit now and it's obvious that you have not been taking care of him. But I figure a person who has a dog this smart must have some good in them, so I have been looking for you."

Lily starts to cry. "I'm so sorry, I will get it together and pick him up later today."

With a serious look on her face, Jonnie lets loose. "What the fuck is wrong with you? Get it together *now*. Look, I could totally get fired for coming to find you. I'm risking my job because your dog deserves better. Are you a fucking bitch or what? I can't stand it, as if your drinking and whatever is an excuse. You reek of alcohol, and you think that's more important than his life? No fucking way! I see this shit all the time. You have a great dog and I couldn't stand by and let him be put down. I've taken buses and walked all over town 'cuz I had to try to find you."

Lily stares at the dirt covering her toes as her feet shift back and forth. She is silent and can't take in all that this woman is telling her.

Jonnie gets right up in her face and screams, "Listen to me! I don't give a flying fuck what happened to you, shitty family, no family or whatever, I don't care. *Don't* have a dog or any animal if you can't take care of him! Don't put your fucked-up life on another living creature. I know what's it's like to be strung out and messed up, and all it is, is selfish. Who the hell do you think you are?"

Two crows fly in and land on the grass right behind Jonnie as Lily tells her again that she is sorry and will pick up Blue after she makes some money.

Jonnie says there isn't time for that. Why she trusts Lily, she has no idea; there's just something about her, so Jonnie says she will loan her the money to bail out Blue. She says they have to go to the shelter now. Lily puts on her sandals and brushes her hair, and Jonnie follows her to her car.

When they get to the shelter, Jonnie says, "If I see Blue here again, I will personally make sure you never get him back. I will find a good home for him and never tell you."

Lily tells Jonnie she will try harder and will pay her back. While Lily is in the restroom, Jonnie remembers that the first time Blue was picked up and brought to the shelter, he looked loved and well cared for. She holds on to that.

When Lily returns, Jonnie says, "Listen to me. Don't *try* harder, just *do* it. Take care of your dog. You obviously love him, so why are you treating him like this? You are killing him."

At the front desk, Jonnie points Lily to the paperwork, which Lily fills out then pays with the money Jonnie gave her. Blue is walked out from the kennels by an attendant leading him with an orange slip collar and Lily sees that he looks awful: he is skin and bones, his coat is patchy, and he has red, infected sores on his back and legs. Lily stares at Blue, frozen and in shock. She falls to her knees and hugs his battered body. Blue is wriggling wildly, happy that Lily has finally come for him.

Through her tears, Lily whispers, "What have I done to you, my prince of princes, my king of kings? Oh my God, what is wrong with me?"

Lightning Strikes

Lily can't believe how Blue looks; she barely recognizes him. She glimpses a reflection of herself and Blue in the shelter window as they leave. She can't fully comprehend what has happened. She wants to fall to her knees and scream as loudly as she can, to rid herself of all the pain she knows is in the world. She is nothing. She is the worst person. This is the nightmare. She is living the horror she allowed to happen. This is not her, but she has done this. If Blue had died because of her stupidity and cruelty, she knows she would have killed herself.

When they get in Homer, Lily starts shaking. Blue sits in the front seat next to her and looks at her with trusting eyes, and something snaps in her right then. All those stupid sayings are true—Like a bolt of lightning striking, Seeing the light at the end of a long dark tunnel—it's happening right now, it's life or death. Lily know she is done. She has to take responsibility for herself and Blue. Her escapist, drugged-out lifestyle needs to end. She has seen herself as the victim, but she now recognizes that Blue is the victim and she is the abuser.

Replaying Jonnie's admonishment about being selfish, she knows it is true. It hits her then and there that she did to Blue what her parents did to her; she abandoned him for her own selfish needs. Lily hugs Blue, whispering in his ear how sorry she is.

Over the next week, Lily doesn't go cold turkey but cuts way back on her drinking and pot smoking and does no partying. Not leaving Blue's side, she takes him to the dog baths and scrubs him clean and puts healing ointment for his sores. Just as when he was a rescued puppy, she feeds him small amounts of healthy food every few hours.

For part of each day, they work their street gig and make decent money. During their first performance Blue tries a few acrobatic flips to see Lily smile but she stops him, noticing that the flips and jumps hurt his weakened body. She invites him to moonwalk, shake hands or howl along with her songs. He is such a ham that even when he cocks his head or walks around the audience, people laugh. Lily hates hearing the whispers and comments about how unhealthy her dog looks. She knows it's true, but Blue is feeling better. His sores are healing and he is putting on weight.

Lily is starting to catch glimmers of her real self, the self that doesn't need to escape. Not a junkie or alcoholic, it's fairly easy for her to stop the drugs and cut way back on her drinking. She doesn't have an addictive personality, she was just running: running from herself, running from her childhood feelings of being unloved.

Ten days later, Lily and Blue drive to the shelter and hand Jonnie an envelope with the money owed and a thank-you letter. In the letter, Lily tells Jonnie what a good person she is for helping Blue, that she will be thankful to her forever, and if there is ever anything Lily can do for her, she will. In large capital letters, she writes, IT'S WAY PAST TIME FOR ME TO GET IT TOGETHER. THANK YOU FOR SAYING IT LIKE IT IS AND SAVING BLUE FOR ME.

Jonnie's gut feelings about Lily were justified and they become fast friends. During the next few weeks, they take Blue on forays to various beaches, shaded hiking trails in the mountains above Felton, and a round-trip hike through the eucalyptus grove at Wilder Ranch. As much a naturalist as Lily if not more, Jonnie likes to identify the animal scat they come across. Coyotes, bobcats, foxes, deer, raccoons, and rabbits are plentiful in the area, as are mountain lions.

Interested, Lily can't help but tease. "So you're a shit inspector, eh?"

"Can't help it, sometimes it's a shitty world and I wanna know where I'm stepping."

Invited to Jonnie's apartment one day, Lily looks around. It's small and extremely neat; plants hang from the ceiling and rest in pots on the floor. Large posters of wild animals cover the walls with African elephants, zebras, lions, gazelles, and giraffes peeking through the hanging greenery. Remembering when they first met and Jonnie moved like an animal Lily couldn't place, now she realizes it is the bent-knee, long stride of a giraffe. Surprising Jonnie with her revelation, they both laugh as Jonnie walks around the apartment exaggerating her giraffe gait.

That afternoon, they take towels and a picnic to Its Beach. Blue plays stick and runs through the small shore waves with two new friends, Elvis, a big dorky black Labrador, and Gretchen, a medium brindle mix of undetermined breeds.

As they watch the dogs play, Jonnie asks, "What are your plans?"

"I have no idea," Lily's mouth is full of a cheese sandwich that she chews before continuing, "other than helping Blue get healthy. And me too. That comes first. What about you?"

"I definitely want to run a shelter one day. It sounds weird to say out loud, but I have found my calling."

"That is so cool, Jonnie, you will be great at that."

"Thanks, I think so too. But all work and no play is not for me. I also want to fall in love."

"That shouldn't be too difficult. You're so beautiful, I bet women fall for you all the time."

"Not that I have noticed, but thanks. I've learned over quite a few relationships that I'm a rescue person—

not only for animals but also people—which doesn't make for lasting relationships. I'm working on it."

They both lay back on their beach towels and silently look at the clouding sky. "There's so much to learn. It's just not that easy being human," Lily quietly muses.

"Damn straight, girl…life can knock ya down, but then we gotta get up."

"With the help of good friends, like you, Jonnie."

"Knock it off, you've thanked me enough."

"No I haven't."

One beer or one pot ciggie a day is all that Lily allows herself. Done with partying, her goal is to quit everything for a couple of months. She wants to find a place where there are no distractions, where she and Blue can swim in fresh water and relax. She pulls a map of northern California from her backpack and shows Jonnie.

"I think it's time for Blue and me to find a place to totally heal. No people, only nature."

Jonnie looks at the maps and points to a place she has been. "It's a little town called Gualala, about an hour south of Mendocino. Just outside the town is a river with areas that are void of tourists and campers. My then-girlfriend and I camped there last summer for two weeks and didn't see another soul. No promises, but I think you and Blue would like it there."

Before leaving Santa Cruz, Lily purchases a bigger tent that she names Big Alice, a new camp stove, a water filter, and plenty of camping supplies and food to live out the rest of the summer. At the art store, she buys six pens and a beautiful turquoise leather-bound notebook. In big letters on the first blank page, she writes, **THE WONDER**. This will be her journal, a private book of thoughts and feelings.

Lily calls Norma to let her know that she and Blue are going north to camp on a river. Not wanting to tell her what almost happened to Blue, she just says she will call from a pay phone every couple of weeks. Norma says she loves her and to take care.

The Gualala River

Just before they reach the town of Gualala, Lily turns right, up into low hills. Traveling through a sparsely inhabited, tree-lined neighborhood, they take the very last turn onto a backwoods dirt road. Homer bumps along until they reach the road's end and park. At the beginning of a seemingly untraveled narrow and dusty trail, they hike across fallen tree stumps and small boulders to the Eden-like campsite beside the river that Jonnie spoke of.

A thick layer of damp fog keeps Blue and Lily cuddled in their sleeping bag most mornings, then Lily lights the camp stove and makes tea for herself and a big pot of oatmeal for both of them. To Blue's breakfast, she adds canned chicken or peanut butter and chopped veggies; to hers, she adds banana and peanut butter. Waiting for the sun to warm the day, Lily reads one of the books she brought or writes in her journal.

Stately and tranquil, the redwoods come right to the water's edge along parts of the river, where soft pink and purple foxglove grow abundant in their shade. Frogs and pollywogs skid and bounce around the shallow water, providing hours of entertainment for Blue. Perched gracefully on logs and rocks along the river, white egrets and blue herons snack on the occasional fish or frog. The river is crystal clear, and just as Jonnie said, Lily hasn't seen another human being.

Every night as the sun gets ready to set, Lily builds a campfire to cook a dinner of noodles or rice and veggies. Blue has kibble with whatever Lily cooks for herself. With no pot or alcohol, Lily is feeling healthier day by day, and tells Blue that her only vice now is her after-dinner hot chocolate. Blue listens intently.

Sometimes Lily plays Magpie and sings by the fire. The simplicity of their days and nights reminds Lily of her first walkabout days. *But it's different now*, she thinks, *something deep inside me has changed*. She wants a healthy life, a good life, and she knows what happens to people who don't get off the escapist merry-go-round of drinking and drugs, like Jewel and Mikey. No matter how much she likes them, they live in their own lies and subterfuge that keeps them from changing. And Mother and Father, their lies weren't about addiction but about themselves.

As the campfire turns to embers, Blue and Lily curl up in Big Alice and listen to the sounds of crickets, owls, and other night creatures until they fall deeply and soundly asleep.

BLUE

Sometimes Lily cries as she talks to me, which is a lot. She is going back over her life and tells me about when she was a child and how lonely she was. I can tell when she is sad, and I crawl in her lap and lick her hand as she pets me. Lily tells me about her parents, how they read books all the time and didn't hug her or talk with her. She tells me that they were "eggheads," which I think sounds delicious, so I start bobbing my head and drooling. Lily laughs and explains that means they were intellectuals. Lily is sad that she doesn't remember her real mother. Truthfully, I don't remember my mother either, or any of my littermates. Lily didn't have any littermates, she is an only child.

My body feels strong again and I can swim and jump and run like a super dog athlete. I know that sounds like bragging, but it's true. I have recuperated quickly with Lily paying all kinds of attention to me. She makes me yummy food and gives me cuddles day and night. She smells good, clean and fresh.

Every day Lily and I swim together, and we have races where she throws sticks and we have to swim super fast to get them. I let Lily win sometimes. She'll hoot and holler no matter which one of us wins, then we race to the shore and do wild dancing in the sand.

. . . .

Early Life

If you want to know more about yourself or your family, you have to be ready to look at the hard stuff, and if you're not ready, it won't come. Lily wasn't ready for years, but with her recent changes and within the silence and peace of camping by the river, she is able to look with fresh eyes at her life with her family.

Books were piled everywhere around her childhood home. Mother read and Father read, usually in their private studies, but sometimes all three would read their separate books in the living room. Lily basked in that time, when every once in a while Mother would say something out loud to Father about what she was reading. Lily thinks Mother wanted her to hear as well.

When Mother was teaching one of her Women in Literature seminars and rereading Jane Austin and modern women writers, she'd say things like, "Did you know that in some parts of the world, women and girls are still not allowed to read or get an education?" or "Did you know that women in the United States only got the right to vote in 1920? And that was only white women. Before that, women were considered men's property. My grandmother was in her twenties then and she was a suffragette, that must have been exciting."

Father would shush her but Mother kept going. "And women were not allowed to inherit property in all states until 1900, and even after that, they couldn't have control over their own finances without their husband's approval. It wasn't until 1970 that women were allowed to have their own credit cards without their husband's signature." Mother put particular emphasis on *1970* as she stared at Father.

Father was Lily's real father and Mother was her stepmother. They were both professors at Occidental College; Father taught philosophy and Mother, literature. They kept their lives private. Gwen, Lily's birth mother, had been a bright, promising grad student of Father's. They had a long-term affair, but when she had a baby, he dumped her. As the story goes, Gwen loved him and thought he would leave his wife and be with her. After Lily was born, Gwen had severe postpartum depression and committed suicide when Lily was five months old. Father had legal rights to Lily.

It's not that Father or Mother wanted her, but they kept her. By the time Lily was six years old she knew, on some level, that she was not wanted. She once tried to make herself invisible by not talking and keeping completely silent for four days, which, sadly enough, her parents didn't acknowledge. She began talking again because one day the squirrels in her backyard ran around so crazy, jumping all over the place, that they made her laugh out loud and she began talking to them. It was as though those squirrels knew Lily when no one else did.

At nine years old, Lily began cutting herself, using scissors to cut crosswise at her wrists. She didn't know why she did it; maybe to prove that she could hurt herself more than her parents hurt her, or maybe because Gwen had killed herself and Lily wanted to know what that felt like. Then again, maybe it was to see if Mother or Father would notice . . . which they never did.

Lily knew that Mother loved Father. It was the way she looked at him, though he paid little attention. Father always had some new student girlfriend and everyone at the college knew about these affairs, including Mother. Father didn't hide it. He spent much time away from the house and didn't engage with his daughter. Angry and unloved by her husband, Mother resented that she had to care for and feed Lily. She would silently press the buttons on the microwave as Lily sat eating alone at the kitchen table. Lily has no memory of Mother eating, only sipping white wine and worrying about adding an ounce to her extra-slim one-hundred-ten-pound frame. That is, until she lay in bed dying and needed Lily to feed her.

When Lily was fourteen, Mother was diagnosed with cancer. Father took Lily out of private high school to be Mother's nursemaid. After her death eight months later, Lily learned that it was Mother who had inherited money from her family and bought their house. A trust lawyer called Lily to come to his office one day. Lily brought Norma with her. She learned that she had inherited money, which was put into a trust. She would receive a small monthly allowance until she turned thirty, at which time she would inherit the full remaining amount. Until then, the lawyer would oversee investing her inheritance money. Father was furious that Mother didn't leave him money but he received the house, which he soon sold to move in with the next new girlfriend. This is when Lily, at fifteen, moved next door to live with Norma.

A butterfly floats and flaps overhead as Lily sprawls in the sun on the riverbank remembering, her feet dipping in the water. Even as Mother lay dying and the cancer quickly spread through her body, she said very little. Lily brought her food and tried to ask questions about her life, but Mother would wave her away with her long, well-manicured fingers or vague responses that meant to leave her alone. The one time she did answer clearly, she said, "Why bother with the questions? I've never wanted to answer them, and I don't have time to do so now. Lily, please hand me my book so I can read a bit."

Tears run down Lily's face as she remembers how alone she felt as a child. Her beloved squirrels and wild birds were really the ones who cared for her and raised her. In elementary school, she was shy and the few friends she made were not allowed to come to her house, as her parents didn't want any of that "childish noise" bothering them. Lily was not permitted to go to friends' houses either, as Mother said something about "keeping their private lives private."

By high school, Lily knew she was different than other kids her age. She felt more connected to the animal world than the human one, and didn't care what others thought. Having lost her shyness by this time, she spoke with everyone, was funny and smart, and did well in class. She didn't particularly care about grades or school and accepted it when Father made her quit her classes to oversee Mother's care. Secretly she hoped Mother would want to talk with her, that they would get to know each other like she and Norma had, but that didn't happen. When Mother died, Lily went to the local public high school. She hung out with friends sometimes like teenagers do, but mostly took pleasure in being home with Norma, having missed so many years of being seen or cared for.

Lily jumps up and runs into the river, splashing water all around. Blue leaps into the water to join the fun and they play their swim and retrieve-stick games until both are panting and out of breath. Back on the river's edge, Lily shakes off her towel and she and Blue lie down to dry off. She grabs The Wonder and writes.

I think I have been living on the edge of my life, hiding behind secrets of secrets and carrying this unknown sadness deep within. Now I see that hiding from others—and more

*importantly, hiding from myself—is self-de-
structive and (as Jonnie said) a selfish thing
to do to another human being or animal. My
guess is that most families have secrets and
it's those unmentionables that lead to dangerous choices and actions. I want my own life. I
want to enjoy my experiences and revel in the
beauty and wonder of this world. I don't want
to live on the edge of my life any more but to
fully embrace it.*

The lid has been lifted from Lily's airtight trunk of denial. She stretches and takes a deep breath as she looks at the slow-moving shallows of the river. An iridescent blue dragonfly hovers and drifts among unseen and mysterious air currents. Lily smiles and writes.

*The river is constant; no matter how deep
or shallow, wide or narrow, as long as there
is water it keeps moving. There are obstacles
like rocks and boulders or sandbars that the
river finds its way around. It can move fast and
wild after a winter storm or, like now, flow slow
and lazy in the warm, dry summer.*

*Life is change, so I need the healing to
continue by being honest with myself. Not taking care of Blue is the worst thing I have ever
done. I have acted thoughtlessly to Norma and
Big Mac, and also to ET. They care about me
and love me and I have not always been kind.
I didn't understand why I abandoned Blue and
everyone who has been so good to me. Now I*

*know that I rejected them because my parents
rejected me.*

. . .

The sun is right overhead, the temperature has spiked, and Lily is sweating. She puts The Wonder away in her tent, chugs water, then whistles for Blue, who is sound asleep in the shade under the nearest redwood tree. He wakes and jogs down to the water, where Lily cuddles him and they enter the river together for a midday bath.

Days turn into weeks and the weeks go past a month. Blue is fit and healthy and Lily is as relaxed as she ever has been. The next time they go into town for supplies, Lily calls Norma and tells her how much she loves it here and how well she and Blue are doing. One day she will bring Norma to this magical part of the river that no one knows about. In about a week they will head back to The Angels.

Before Lily hangs up, she tells Norma she loves her and appreciates all she has done for her. Surprised by Lily's openness, Norma thanks her and says she loves her too.

The Dark of Night

At twilight, when the light of day, moment by moment, treads into the dark of night, Lily and Blue sit quietly at the edge of the river. It's the time of day when the possibility of the dog turning into the wolf scrapes our minds. It's the bewitching hour, that tick-tock of time when fear lurks at the doorstep, wondering whether to enter. Lily is used to this feeling, this end of daylight and switch to darkness; she has lived outside for too long to succumb to fear. It's another beautiful night on the Gualala River. The sky has turned a dark phthalo blue with small, folded pockets of light forming a pattern she has never seen before.

Blue and Lily have not been sleeping in Big Alice lately, as the weather is warm and Lily likes to watch the stars as she falls asleep. She plays a couple of Woody Guthrie songs to Blue, the campfire burns low, and they cuddle in her sleeping bag for a good night's sleep.

BLUE

I wake to the smell of burger meat and hot dogs not too far away. The night is dark with just a sliver of moon and Lily is gently snoring. I don't want to wake her, so I creep off quietly to investigate the yummy smells. I find fresh meat and hot dogs a ways down the river. There is another smell there too, but I can't place it. I am chowing down on a couple of large mouthfuls when I hear Lily's shrill cry, "BLUE!"

It chills me to my bones. I race to her as fast as I can. As I get closer, I can't separate Lily from the huge shape on top of her. I recognize the smell that was near the meat and hear a man's voice. My heart is thundering in my chest. I know something bad is happening to Lily.

I jump on the shape that is covering her and bite down hard. My teeth dig in. The man yells as I hold on tight to what I think is his shoulder. He jumps up and tries to strike me. He is flailing all around, trying to get me off his back, but I am determined, my jaws locked on him.

· · · · · · ·

The slap to my face comes hard and fast and jolts me from sleep. I reflexively scream, but no noise comes out as a heavy hand grips against my mouth. Another hand tears off my t-shirt and sweatpants. A man's voice growls, "You fucking bitch, you piece of shit. I'll rock your world then cut you from here to there, you lying cunt."

It feels like I'm being ripped apart. The pain is nauseating. I am a bird being broken into pieces by an alien giant. Where is Blue? Has the man killed him? I can't breathe, I have to get his hand off my mouth. When he finishes, he flips me over and his hand leaves my mouth for a second. I scream, "BLUE!" as loud as I can, but it is more like a strangled screech.

The man hits me hard on the side of my face as he grabs me from behind. He breathes heavily while whispering in my ear, "Shut up, bitch, you are gonna die. you're not the first and you won't be the last."

His breath is rancid and his body stinks. I always sleep with the gun under my pillow since ET gave it to me, but I can't move. His weight is excruciating and his hands around my neck are choking me. My body begins to go limp. Just then, I hear a deep growl and the man yells and jumps back. Blue has bought me half a second. I grab the gun. Everything happens so fast, I can barely see. The man is howling, and I hear a yelp and a thud. Is that Blue being hurled to the ground? All is hazy, but I think I see the large shape of the man right next to me. In that second, I shoot toward him, and as I pull the trigger I hear ET's voice in my head: "Shoot three times, always shoot three times."

I do, but don't know if I hit him or not. I am not sure of what I am seeing. My heart and head pound as I whirl around, elbows locked with arms stretched in front of me, the gun ready to shoot again. I see what I think is the man slumped on the ground. I poke the shape with my foot as I point the gun right at him. He is quiet and unmoving. Is he dead or just trying to trick me? Where is Blue? I keep the gun pointed at the bulky shape on the ground and feel around my sleeping bag for the flashlight. Shining it at the dark shape, I see it is the man and kick him hard but he doesn't move. Blood is everywhere. I look closer. His head is oddly angled to the side. I don't know if he is dead or just really hurt. His ugly face is staring at me and I hesitate for a second, then shoot him in the face.

I shine the flashlight all around and find Blue a few feet away, not moving. I touch him and can feel him breathing. I whisper his name and direct the flashlight to his body to see where he is hurt. There is blood around his mouth but nowhere else. I gently touch him again, and all of a sudden he jerks his head up and growls, baring his teeth as if he is going to attack. I yell, "Blue, it's me."

He recognizes me and stops, whimpers, then screams loudly, almost like a person. I hold him close while we both cry and shake together. I aim the flashlight again at the dead man, around the campsite, and closely on Blue's body and my own. I touch my face and feel that I am bleeding from my nose and mouth as well as down below. My whole body hurts and I can't stop shaking. The man is sprawled out, a huge lump of nothing on the forest floor. Bone pieces and body tissue lie scattered around what used to be his head and blood is soaking into the earth. I don't want to look at him, but I need to make sure he doesn't move.

I grab my blanket, and Blue and I crawl a few yards away. I wrap the blanket around us both. My back against a redwood tree, I hold the gun pointed right in front of us. I talk softly to Blue and hold him as we wait for darkness to fade into the shadows of morning.

I am alive. Blue is alive. We are bruised, bloodied and beaten, but we're here. Blue saved my life. I am in shock, and thoughts keep tumbling through my mind. I should go into town and tell the police what happened, take Blue to the veterinarian and me to the doctor. Then I think of all the questions the police might ask. What are we doing camping alone? Did you pick up this guy at a bar in town? What am I doing with an unregistered gun? Would they impound Blue or even euthanize him because he attacked the man?

I don't know anyone in town. I don't know who this man is. He may be local and not seem to be a rapist and murderer to the people here. What if he is a policeman or someone in a powerful position? I realize that I know nothing about this place. I look at Blue and make my decision.

Aftermath

As soon as daylight emerges, Blue and Lily walk down to the river to wash as best they can. Lily fills the teakettle and builds up the fire, gets dressed, packs up Big Alice and all their belongings, and carries them to Homer. It takes many trips and Lily's body is in pain. She keeps out the poop shovel and the heavy rope clothesline.

Going back to the body, she pours the boiling water on the man's fingertips, ties the rope around his ankles, and drags him as far into the forest as she can, which is only a few feet, as dead weight is very heavy. The mostly sandy soil makes it easy enough to dig a trench, and Lily rolls him into the hole. Lily knows that she and Blue need to get out of there, but she has to make his body disappear for as long as possible.

She hopes hungry wild animals will find him before people do. She scoops up the bloody bits with the shovel and tosses them into the pit. It's barely deep enough but will have to do. She shovels sandy dirt to cover the body and drags fallen tree branches to lay on the excavated dirt.

"Fuck you, I'm glad you are dead," Lily says as eulogy to the freshly dug grave.

She uses a leaf-covered branch to sweep the entire area, dismantles the fire pit, and scatters the rocks and burned wood into the river. She picks up the shell casings, fills the holes the tent stakes have made, and makes sure there are no hidden scraps of paper, dog treats, food or clothes around. After double-checking to make sure there is no trace of their campsite, Blue and Lily walk as quickly as they can back to Homer over the patchwork ground of pine needles, twigs, tree roots, soil and leaves.

They are both limping and exhausted, but they have to get on the road. Luckily Homer has plenty of gas and they head south out of town. Near Santa Rosa, Lily looks for a clean, cheap motel along the freeway, to check their injuries more carefully and take a hot shower. As she drives, her thoughts jump around and she goes over details of the campsite to make sure she didn't forget anything. She whispers to no one, "Why did I pour boiling water on that man's fingertips? Probably saw it on some stupid TV show."

Considering the daylight vision of using the poop shovel to collect pieces of that man's blown-apart face, she whispers, "Crazy."

Blue looks anxiously at Lily and she pets his head. Her heart races, and like the dead man's body waiting to be discovered, she can feel panic hiding just around the corner. She mumbles, "Not now, Lily, pay attention to the road and breathe."

At the motel, the woman behind the counter glances at Lily and asks with a concerned look, "Are you all right?"

"I know, I look awful. I was in a friend's car and we got in an accident down by San Francisco. I've been to the doctor and I'm fine," Lily lies. She doesn't want the woman to know where she came from or where she's heading, and the story just falls out of her mouth.

The woman asks, "How is your friend?"

"She's fine too, but looks about the same as me."

"Let me know if you need anything."

"Thank you," Lily responds. "I just need quiet and rest before I head north."

Lily parks Homer right in front of the room, grabs her bag, and she and Blue hasten inside. Ugly but comforting motel decor greets them. Lily glances at the tired geometric-patterned bedspread and faded framed prints of the Sonoma wine country. Dumping her bag on the bed, she heads straight for the bathroom, turns on the shower and strips off her clothes, with Blue right beside her. Gingerly she lifts him into the shower tub and gently washes him.

They stay in the room and hobble around in pain for a couple of days. Lily's bruises are very dark, with discoloration and swelling on her face and neck. Blue has swelling along one side of his body. She feeds him baby aspirin every couple of hours and doses herself as well. Lily calls Norma on the second day and asks if she can put the motel charges on her credit card, and Norma agrees. Not wanting Norma to worry, Lily waits to tell her what happened, saying they will be home in a couple of days. Stifling her many questions, Norma simply answers, "I look forward to seeing you both."

BLUE

I can't stop panting. When we arrive at a motel, Lily checks us into a room. Inside, she carefully touches my whole body and moves everything this way and that way. It hurts, but not too badly. She takes me into the shower with her and washes me very carefully with soap, then rinses me really well. She rubs me dry with the motel towels, puts me on the bed, and tells me to sleep while she showers. Lily is in the shower a long time. When she comes out wrapped in a towel, she crawls in bed with me. She lies there staring at the ceiling and holds me.

Eventually Lily gets up and dresses. She goes out to Homer and brings in food and supplies. She makes a really good meal of peanut butter sandwiches, yogurt, a banana, dog biscuits and almond milk. Lily turns on the TV and we watch the news and a nature show about wild animals. We both fall asleep, but I am awakened later by Lily crying. She is sobbing and can't stop. I lick her face and lean my body against hers. She kisses me and I fall asleep again. When I wake later, Lily is sleeping, so I watch her and wait.

· · · · · · ·

On the drive to Norma's, Lily asks Blue , "Do you mind stopping in Pismo for a little beach walk? It will be good to breathe the ocean air. We have been cooped up inside for days. I have enough money to get us some fish and chips too, okay buddy?"

Lily is already planning how to move past what they went through. She doesn't want to become afraid of being in the world. Lily glances over at Blue, seeing his love-dog eyes and the cigarette burn scars he got as a puppy. She knows his life has been an act of will, with his heart leading the way. Aloud she says, "It's time for *my* act of will. I am going to make sure we move beyond this." Gently touching Blue's head, she whispers, "You are my angel dog, Blue, my prince of princes, my king of kings."

In Pismo Beach Lily purchases an order of fish and chips and carries it to the edge of the water. As they sit on the sand, she feeds Blue the fish one piece at a time and lunches on the French fries. When they are done, Lily walks a short distance barefoot in the flat, shallow water, breathing in the cloudless sky and crisp, cool air while looking out to sea. With Blue walking slowly beside her, they head back to Homer and continue their drive to The Angels.

Blue and Lily arrive at Norma's quiet and subdued. At first glance Norma knows something has happened; they seem shell-shocked, and not for one second will Blue take his eyes off Lily as he follows her, limping from room to room. Deep purple bruises are apparent around Lily's face and neck. Norma hasn't seen Lily and Blue in a long time, but she knows to wait until Lily is ready to share with her. Norma prepares a dinner of vegetarian lasagna and green salad, and a hamburger and zucchini stew to add to Blue's kibble. She puts Blue's bowl on the floor right by them in the living room while they silently watch TV.

Most of the next day is lost to sleep. Late in the afternoon, Lily and Blue shuffle from the cottage to join Norma in the main house. She is on the sofa, flipping through a magazine, trying not to ask the obvious questions. As soon as Lily sits, she breaks down sobbing. Norma moves closer to put her arm around her, and Lily slowly tells of the assault and the aftermath. Blue crawls up to lie on Lily's lap with his head on Norma's knee. The story is far beyond anything Norma could ever have imagined.

Early the next morning, Norma calls her doctor and makes an appointment for Lily. Over breakfast they discuss what she will want to say to explain the bruising. Lily has already thought about this. She tells Norma about a woman she met in Santa Cruz who was into orgies, and how once she was bruised all over for many days. Lily is prepared to say something like that, if the doctor asks. Norma also makes an appointment with the veterinarian who has known Blue since he was a puppy. They think Blue's injuries will be easy enough to explain, if necessary, with a story about a hiking fall.

The doctor asks a few questions, but nothing that Lily has to lie about. She gives Lily a prescription for antibiotics and a pregnancy test—just in case—and tells her it will take a bit of time for her to physically heal, but not to worry. Then she says, "Lily, if you ever want to talk about anything, give me a call."

Blue has aged a lot since the veterinarian last saw him more than two years ago. She tells Lily that he appears much older than his five years. Though Blue is deeply bruised, nothing is broken and he will recover, but he should take it easy from now on. Seeing the worried look in Lily's eyes, she explains that dogs who have been severely abused as puppies, as Blue was, are prone to health issues as they get older. They may need extra care as they age. Lily lets the vet know that she understands.

When they get back home, they go for an easy walk in the neighborhood. Blue pees as high as he can on almost every tree trunk, telling the neighborhood dogs that he is back. Norma and Lily quietly walk beside each other.

The End of Secrets

Over the next weeks and months, Lily loses her previous need for secrecy. There is new clarity and a matter-of-factness about her. She tells Norma everything that happened on the Gualala River and in Santa Cruz. She even tells her about being so fucked up that Blue almost got euthanized at the county shelter.

Later that week when Norma returns home from work, Lily asks her to come into the garden. As she sits down, Lily says, "Norma, I have been thinking again about how, after I shot that man and he appeared to be dead, I shot him again directly in his face. Am I weird or crazy to have done that? Is there something wrong with me?"

Thinking for a moment, Norma replies, "It does sound extreme, like in that moment maybe a rage took hold of you, or in that moment you had to make sure, be *certain*, that he was dead. I have no idea what I would have done, I can't begin to imagine, but I doubt I would have been as brave as you. Lily, that may have been the best thing to do, given the situation."

Lily takes Norma's hand. "Thank you."

Norma replies, "Honey, you are here and so is Blue. That means that you did a lot right."

Waking the next morning, Lily creeps out of bed, trying not to disturb Blue, who is sleeping with his head on her pillow and his body under the covers. He looks so cute that she wants to kiss him on his forehead but she doesn't want to wake him. Tip-toeing to the bathroom to pee, she wipes herself and sees blood. *Good,* she thinks, *my second period in the last eight weeks since the attack. Good.*

Staring at her face in the mirror, she whispers, "Shit, that was insane. That man was disgusting, horrid, a monster. He was looking for someone and I was there. It was just bad timing and had nothing to do with me. I killed a man and I don't have any remorse. That may be crazy but it's true. And he will NEVER do that to anyone else again, that's good to know. And weird as it is, I'm okay."

She takes a deep breath, leans over the sink to be closer to the mirror, and questions herself. "Are you *really* okay? You have been pretty fucked up in your life and didn't exactly know it, so are you really okay?" She stands back and takes a general look at herself. "I'm okay. I don't feel fucked up, I feel happy."

Lily crawls back in bed with Blue. As he awakens, she cuddles him and asks if he is okay. He thumps his tail under the covers. It's clear to Lily that if she didn't have Blue and a gun, she would be dead. *In the natural world of animals, sometimes it is kill or be killed, it's part of nature. I needed to survive.* However, the surprise and violence of the attack has affected her. She decides to carry a cell phone, her walks with Blue are only along busier parks and pathways, and she is more conscious of who is around.

One Sunday, Lily asks Norma to help her with an online search. She has been thinking about what that man said to her, about her not being the first or the last. She's concerned that other women in that area were murdered by the same man before her own attack. In their online newspaper investigation, they find four women who went missing in the last year. Only their names, dates, and the location of last sightings are available. Though they may be victims of the same man, Lily and Norma don't know what to do with this information. For now, they write the women's names in a notebook. As part of their search, they scan newspaper articles for a man's body discovered along the Gualala River but find nothing.

Lily has told Norma everything about her time living in Santa Cruz, her drug and alcohol misadventures, and her time with ET. Lily wants to know what Norma thinks of smoking pot or doing other drugs, and asks if Norma has ever gone off the deep end into anything illicit or self-destructive.

Norma laughs. "Lily, I am from a very Catholic family. I feel guilty even having a glass of wine, which is ridiculous since the priests drink. But truthfully, I was a good girl who followed the rules. Well . . . except for sex."

Lily's eyes open wide. "Okay Norma, spill the beans, what did you do?"

Norma laughs some more. "Having sex before marriage is frowned on by the church, but once I got to college I fooled around a lot."

Lily has wondered. "With girls or boys?"

"Both. I was with boys first because I thought that was the only option, then I met Ginny. She was in my sociology class and we hit it off. I never told my parents, that would have been too much for them. My mother may have understood, but I didn't want to risk it."

"What happened to Ginny?"

"We were together about a year and then it just fizzled out, like many relationships."

Norma looks closely at Lily and thinks this is the right time to ask. "So Lily, how are you feeling these days, sexually, after the attack? I know you and Big Mac talk on the phone sometimes, anything else going on?"

Lily smiles, as she hasn't said much about Big Mac and knows Norma is fishing. "There isn't much to tell. I called Mac a couple of weeks ago to say hi and we have talked a few times. He's seeing someone, but he says it isn't serious. He clearly doesn't trust me and told me how hurt he was when I left. I totally get it, I wouldn't trust me either. There's a connection for sure, but I don't know what will happen. We're just talking."

"You know, Lily, sometimes broken hearts don't heal, and you did break his heart. Mac was devastated when you left. I'm just saying, don't be surprised if he decides that he doesn't want to see you."

"Norma, that may be true, and if it is, I'll totally understand, but maybe he will only have the leftover scars of a broken heart." Lily smiles sadly. "I think my broken heart scars help me to love more, and frankly I don't know what I can do about hurting him the way I did. I guess we'll see if he can forgive me."

She is silent for a while, then says, "About sex, I am not sure. You know I've slept with a lot of guys, all of that was my choice, and maybe it was a bit fucked up because I was super loaded with many of them, but it was never violent. Sometimes I didn't even know their name and I didn't care 'cuz it didn't mean anything. That may not be very nice, but that was the way it was."

Lily stands, circles the room, then sits again. "The assault was awful but it wasn't sex, it was abuse of the worst kind. I was nothing to him other than a woman to torture and kill for his own twisted need. It had nothing to do with me."

Pulling her hair back to re-clip it in a loose ponytail, Lily says, "Truthfully, I have no idea how I will act or react when the time comes, but I know I am done with casual sex, at least for now. The next time I have sex it will be with someone I trust and am interested in."

"That sounds very healthy and thoughtful." Norma is touched. "Thank you for telling me this and letting me be a part of your life."

Lily jumps up from her seat and hugs Norma. "Are you kidding? I am totally the lucky one, you have saved me."

• • •

It started with a few sporadic phone calls, then short check-ins, evolving over the last month into long, chatty, hard-to-hang-up calls. Lily tells Mac in one of their first phone conversations that she is no longer drinking and drugging, maybe a glass of wine or beer every once in a while, but that's all. She apologizes for walking out on him and explains that back then she was running, not from him, but herself. Mac doesn't respond, he just listens.

In a couple months, Mac invites Lily to see *Manchester by the Sea*, a movie playing nearby. He has read the reviews and tells Lily it may be depressing.

"Good," Lily responds, "I love depressing movies."

Lily cries pretty much through the whole movie and Mac cries some too. As they walk down the block to get smoothies, they are silent. The movie was too heavy for this first face-to-face meeting in almost five years, but it's obvious to both of them that something is there. They are cautious together. Lily apologizes again for walking out.

Mac looks at her. "I hate to keep saying this, but you really hurt me when you left. I don't know if I can trust you again, and if I do, it may take a long time."

"I totally understand, and there is no hurry. Maybe you will learn to trust me, but no matter what, I hope we can be friends."

When Lily gets home that night, she tells Norma, "Mac seems really good. He loves his work and looks pretty much the same, only less wrinkled and kind of stylish. He says he needs the film industry directors and producers to take him seriously. I think the feelings are there, but they may not lead anywhere."

Heron's Roses

For the first time ever, Lily questions Norma about her childhood and family. Over an afternoon, with many cups of tea, a walk with Blue, and more tea, Norma tells her own family saga.

"My mother was born in Española, New Mexico. Both my mother's parents were immigrants from Mexico, and her father, my grandfather, was a business owner of some kind. Growing up, my mother had two sisters and a brother. My mother's parents were very strict. One of her sisters, Lucia, ran away when she was a teenager and got in a lot of trouble and died fairly young. Her brother Raoul got drafted at eighteen and went to Vietnam and was killed in the war."

"That is so sad, Norma," Lily mutters.

"I never knew them, but yes, it is sad. My mother's oldest sister Maria, ten years older, got married and moved to Florida with her husband. As the youngest, my mother stayed at home and took care of her parents. She became a teacher and eventually met my father when he came to fix the plumbing at the school. It was love at first sight.

Norma goes to the kitchen to make tea. Lily follows, reaching for the teapot and cups while Norma lights the stove under the kettle and continues, "My father was very handsome and funny. Being from a poor family, he had very little schooling. When I was a teenager, Dad told me that he fell in love with my mother not for her beauty, but for her smarts. Smiling his broad smile, he said he knew he would need a full-time teacher for the rest of his life. Mom was in the room and I remember my parents looking at each other, eyes sparkling as they both giggled. It was so cute, they really loved each other.

"They married the next summer, and later that year, my grandfather died. Hoping for better-paying jobs, my parents moved to Los Angeles and took my grandmother with them. Dad worked for a plumbing company for a few years, then started his own business. My mother found a good teaching job and eventually they bought their house in Echo Park. I came along the next year. My grandmother, whom I called Nini, took care of me when my parents worked. My brother was born three years later."

Listening intently, Lily blurts, "You have a brother?"

"I did, but only for a couple of years. As a baby

he was diagnosed with leukemia and he died when he was two. I kind of remember him, but mostly through photos. My parents were devastated, but they were very religious and believed that if God needed Roberto, it was His way."

"I am so sorry, Norma. What about your Nini, what happened to her?"

"She was very 'Old World" she wore all black every day after her husband died and never learned English. I remember her bedroom was always immaculate. She had a single bed with an old crucifix above it, a wooden straight-backed chair, and a hand-carved dresser with old photographs on top. The largest one was of my grandfather in his business suit. There was another photo of them on their wedding day, one of Raoul in his army uniform, a photo of my mom when she graduated from teachers' college, a baby photo of me, and another photo of my mom and dad with me as a little girl, holding Roberto when he was just born. The positions of the photos never changed and not a bit of dust was allowed to collect on them.

"Nini doted on me and taught me to sew, cook and clean, everything I needed to know to be a good Mexican wife. She read her Bible every day and walked to the Catholic church around the corner every morning. I went to church on weekends with her and my parents. Nini died of a stroke when I was fourteen. I still miss her."

Lily gets up, gives Norma a hug, goes in the kitchen and brings back a plate of chocolate chip cookies she baked the day before. She asks, "So what about your parents? You never mention them."

"Honey, you've never asked."

Lily has a hurt expression. "Norma, I think I've been lost inside. I'm sorry for being so self-involved."

"No worries, it seems that you are making more room every day for everything and everyone. This may sound harsh, but I was not going to share my story with you until you asked. Curiosity about another person's life is a gift one gives, so now I can gift back to you, Lily, by telling you my story."

"I never thought of it that way, but that makes sense. Will you continue?"

"Yes, of course. I was a good student, like you. And like you, being an only child for most of my life, I didn't play with friends very often. After school every day I would sit at the kitchen table and do my homework as Nini read her Bible. The funny thing was that Nini would only read the Bible for about a minute, then she would pull a paperback from her apron pocket and switch to one of the trashy Mexican novels that were her only vice. She never read one of those books in front of my parents, which made me feel very special. While reading, Nini would screech and snort and say all kinds of phrases in Spanish that meant, "Oh I can't read this!" or, "Oh no, this is too much." She kept reading while she closed and opened the book over and over again and crossed herself. I would tease her and we would laugh together."

Getting up, they walk out to the patio. The sweet scent of roses fills the air as they stretch out on the lounge chairs. Blue follows and lies on the ground.

"We had no relatives near, as my father had been an orphan and had no family, and my mother's only other family was her sister who lived in Florida. Nini and my mother never went to see Maria and Maria never came to see them. Something must have happened between them but I never knew what. I never met Maria, but whatever it was, the argument had to be pretty bad, because my mother was an extremely thoughtful and forgiving person.

"She was also a modern Americanized woman. Community oriented and political, she helped a lot of people in our neighborhood, which was filled with gang members when I was growing up. Besides her teaching job, which she loved, she helped with church functions and started a food program for kids in the neighborhood. She rarely did housework because Nini did it, and when Nini died, I took that over. When my mother died, hundreds of people came to honor her. I am sure I became a teacher because of her."

With tears in her eyes, Norma stands. "Let's get some exercise before I tell you about my dad, and what happened next."

Lily, tearing up as well, says, "I'm sure I would have loved your mother. I am so sorry, you must miss her all the time."

"I do. Come on Blue, let's go for a walk."

BLUE

Lily, Norma, and I go to the park. They continue talking and on and off, they cry. I don't listen much because the air is warm and there's birdsong from almost every tree. The lawn has been mowed and the air is pungent with the warm, grassy aroma. My body feels strong as I strut and prance along the trail, looking quite handsome, if I say so myself.

The smell of two new dogs in the neighborhood assaults my nose as I sniff various tree trunks. One is a big male, definitely taller than I am, and the other one is a small and active little pisser. Every day the canine pee-mail system informs me as to what I need to know. Most humans are oblivious to this, but not Lily. Sometimes she says, "Well, my little prince, which dog's smell is the most intoxicating to you today?" Lily is so smart.

• • • • • • •

As they walk along, Lily says, "I want to hear about your dad. Your parents sound really in love, this is so romantic."

"Very romantic, Lily, and as with some love stories, a bit heartbreaking. I may cry a little when I tell you, I hope that is okay."

Before Norma has time to say anything else, Lily gets tears in her eyes, then Norma tears up and they both laugh at what sob sisters they are. Blue looks up for a second, then goes back to sniffing.

"My dad's name was Heron."

"What a beautiful name," Lily interrupts.

"Yes, Heron Rodriguez Plumbing was the name of his business, he was so proud. Growing up in an orphanage, he never dreamed he could achieve what he did. Here he was married to his beloved Linda, he bought a house and built his own business, he was the American Dream in person."

Hearing a siren wailing in the distance, Norma stops for a moment. They go up the hill to a bench among the dry brush and grasses, sit and overlook the roofs and streets of Eagle Rock.

Norma takes a deep breath. "After Nini died it was just the three of us. Dad spent his time after work puttering around the house and garden, repairing every little thing. A natural gardener, his roses were his favorites, and he would sing and talk to them like they were his babies. Cutting the most precious, he would make a bouquet and present them to my mother. One time I watched him get on one knee and with the biggest smile I ever saw, hand the bouquet to her, saying, 'My beautiful Linda, my queen, may I, a lowly peasant, present my bag of gold to you?' She laughed and took his flowers and his other hand. As he stood, she said, 'You are my king, my love.' She placed the roses in a special vase in the middle of the dining table. The roses in our garden are his, I moved them here when I sold the house."

Lily makes a mental note to research rose gardening so she can help take care of Heron's roses.

"One day Dad noticed a few shingles were loose on the roof and went up to fix them. We don't know what happened, but the doctor thinks he had a heart attack and fell off the roof. I was at City College at the time, but Mom was in the kitchen when she heard a big crash. He remained in a coma for a few days, then died. Both Mom and I were there, holding his hands. He died peacefully, which was a comfort.

"Mom was so sad and had a hard time for a while. Remember I told you about her being what she called 'locked in', and asking me to hug her and then give her a push?"

Lily nods yes.

"Then she got busy and basically started a whole new life. When she passed years later, I sold their house, bought this house, and met you."

Lily touches Norma's hand. "You must have felt so sad and alone, after losing all that love."

"That's true, Lily, but my Nini told me when I was a teenager that feeling sad is okay. She said that sadness allows one to open their heart to more joy. You know, when I met you, Lily, you filled some of the sadness in my heart."

BLUE

We have been living in the garden cottage at Norma's for what seems a long time and I am very happy. We all are. Most mornings Lily reads or writes in her

journal while I lie next to her. Or I wander around the garden while she waters plants and fills the bird feeders. In the afternoon I go over to Norma's while Lily volunteers at the animal shelter. When she comes home, she sits on the floor in front of me so I can smell all the animals she visited. It's very exciting, and I know when I am done sniffing that it will be dinnertime.

I do volunteer work as well. My favorite job is to keep the kitchen floors clean at both my houses. Using my tongue as a mop works wonders on any spilled bits of food. Sometimes I lick the bird poop off the patio. If Lily catches me she tells me to stop, but in my defense, humans have no idea how tasty bird shit is to a dog.

· · · · · · ·

The Second Time Around

More than ten months have passed since the attack on the Gualala River and Lily is ready to take her freedom back. Feeling healthy and strong, she wants to make sure she can still feel safe while traveling. She plans a road trip to Santa Cruz to visit Jonnie. She and Blue will sleep in Homer and will even try entertaining on the streets. Lily has saved her monthly trust payments, so she has money for an emergency and will call or text Norma from her cell phone every day. Looking forward to some of her favorite hikes and beaches, Lily contacts Jonnie and they make a date to meet on the grassy hill along the San Lorenzo River.

Before leaving, Lily goes to see her favorite dog at the shelter, who will probably be adopted before Lily returns. She has named her Angelica, "of the angels", as she was found wandering the streets of downtown Los Angeles. A bloodhound mix, she is lean and leggy, black and tan with long, droopy ears and short fur. Her sad eyes have seen a lot in her few years. Lily walks her on the sidewalk around the shelter, where she is learning to be good on leash. Still somewhat fearful of men, she has a sweet disposition and wants to please. Lily thinks Angie will find a home soon.

• • •

Arriving in Santa Cruz late in the morning, Lily is thirsty for the latte she used to order at their favorite cafe. As soon as they walk in, Blue remembers the treats the baristas fed him. He goes to the counter and sits waiting. Annie is still working there; she says hi to Lily and comes around the counter with lots of treats in her hand. "Blue, you look so handsome, I have missed you!" She gives him a hug and hands him one treat after another, and Blue wags his tail after each treat.

Lily smiles and orders her latte and a grilled cheese sandwich. Looking around, she can't believe who she sees at a back table.

"Hi, Josh. How ya doin'?"

"What? Josh replies.

Lily says loudly, "How are you? Long time no see."

Looking up, his dark eyes squinting, he remembers their affair. She looks healthy, still hot looking, that hippie kind of hot, but he doesn't want to be bothered. He mumbles something incoherent and turns back to his computer screen. Josh keeps an imaginary Rolodex file in his head that keeps people under G for good or F for fucked up. He placed Lily under F a long time ago, when he got home from work one day and she had moved out without a goodbye.

Registering his coldness, Lily sees the puka shell necklace and gold chain he's sporting with his dark blue "Namaste" t-shirt. She holds back a chuckle and offers, "Okay Josh, I get it, I was a total shit to you, but you were an ass too. Believe it or not, it's good to see you." She waits a few seconds and adds, "I'm sorry I was so fucked up."

Josh looks up, eyes hooded, and flicks his hand in a dismissive wave. Through the grapevine, Lily's heard that Josh has been with Marnie for the past year or so. They are into their expensive bikes and being Mr. and Mrs. Yoga. She met Marnie at various parties way back when and remembers that she mostly talked about herself and was not "street" at all. Lily thinks they probably make a good couple.

"Bye Josh." Lily waves as she picks up her latte and the grilled cheese sandwich, which she shares with Blue at an outside table. The smell of honeysuckle floats gently on the light breeze. A narrow strip of planted soil between the parking lot and picnic tables is alive with bees nursing on purple and blue salvias. As Lily breathes in the dusty warm scent of sage, she texts Norma to let her know all is fine.

Blue hops into Homer's backseat and Lily decides they will hike up at Fall Creek, a popular hiking path in

Felton. The dirt trail meanders through a redwood forest along a narrow creek. The air is lush and moist, and though no dogs are allowed, there are plenty of local hikers with their dogs. This is the Santa Cruz she loves; people smile and say hello and ask about each other's dogs. They stop at the little organic market in town to get snacks and sandwich-making supplies for an easy car camping dinner. That night, after watching a brilliant golden-orange sunset over the bay, Lily and Blue have a restful night's sleep in Homer.

"Good morning my little prince, do you want to work the streets today? Let's get gussied up and go to our old place on Pacific Avenue and see if we can make some money."

Blue licks Lily's face in agreement, hoping breakfast is first, which it is.

At the public bathroom, from the well-used and well-loved patchwork backpack ET gave her years ago, Lily pulls out a ziplock bag with toothbrush, toothpaste, washcloth, and soap. Blue gets a wet down and serious paper towel dry to shine his short, black-and-white coat. Lily then fills the small white porcelain sink and washes herself, brushes her teeth, and spends a bit of time brushing the knots from her night-slept hair.

BLUE

Yummy like a freshly sliced apple, the air smells delicious. All clean and lying outside the bathroom door, I watch the world as I wait for Lily to finish getting

ready. Busy blackbirds hop from branch to branch on a pine tree growing nearby while tiny insects crisscross the ground at my paws. I scoop up a few ants with my tongue just to see what they taste like—not bad—so I lick the ground a few more times. Lily exits the bathroom, sees what I am doing and admonishes, "Blue, don't lick the ground, silly dog!"

I sheepishly smile at the vision of her, wearing a blue camisole top and floral skirt, her feet hidden in cowgirl boots that clip-clop along the ground as we walk. Later Lily will put wildflowers in her hair. She tells me that she is plain, so she needs to dress up a bit for work.

"The chestnut trees are looking quite cheerful today," Lily says as we walk down Pacific Avenue. I look at their large, flat, hand-shaped leaves that shade parts of the sidewalk and stop to sniff the variety of dog pee at the base of each tree. Finding the perfect place, I take a quick leak on one of the sturdy trunks.

Shoppers and tourists browse window displays of latest fads and eye candy. A woman carrying her small baby in a front pack talks on her cell phone as the baby sleeps soundly snuggled against her mother's heartbeat.

Lily and I set up for our work day, which means I lie around while Lily unfolds her street chair and takes Magpie from its case. As she tunes up, I mindlessly scratch behind my ear until I notice a dragonfly sipping nectar from a jasmine vine in front of a shop nearby. I furtively creep over to try to catch and eat it, but Lily gives me one of her looks that

means I need to lie down again. I plop down right next to her, my head resting on my front paws. Before I know it, Lily puts the fringed leather cowboy vest on me. "Here we go, Blue, let's have some fun."

This means I gotta make us some money.

. . . .

Blue is adorable, working the crowd as he prances around and sits to shake hands with the tourists. He does his Michael Jackson moonwalk imitation, slowly walking backwards one paw at a time while he gently sways his body. Lily sings Bob Dylan's classic, "Blowin' in the Wind" and after the last line, "The answer, my friend, is blowin' in the wind, the answer is blowin' in the wind," Blue ends the show with a long, mournful howl.

A musical throwback to the sixties and seventies, Lily's best street songs are by Joni Mitchell, Pete Seeger and Bette Midler, but her favorite singer is Amy Winehouse. Lily is her same age and loves her voice and original style, but she has no illusions and knows her vocal limitations. She would never try to sing Amy's songs on the street.

Today the audience keeps growing, they laugh and clap and drop lots of money into Midas, Lily's money can. Blue goes through the crowd to receive many head pets, as he knows he's the star of the show. In three hours they make ninety-two dollars, mostly ones and fives, but Lily also counts a ten and a twenty. She smiles at their success.

Grabbing their gear, Lily and Blue walk to Homer, dump their stuff in the back, and drive to Trader Joe's. She asks Blue what he wants, as he has to wait in Homer while she shops. He nods his boxy head a few times and licks his lips before he moves to the driver's seat to look out the window and wait patiently for Lily's return.

She walks out of TJ's with the cart full. Just for Blue: dog kibble, canned salmon, canned chicken, peanut-butter dog biscuits. For both to share: peanut butter, whole wheat bread, provolone and cheddar cheeses, carrots, celery, apples, bananas, a mango, two avocados, and lots of bottled water. For the crows and squirrels that may visit them at the river or Lighthouse Field: a bag of peanuts in the shell. And just for Lily: yogurt, cashews, organic snack bars and almond milk. Lily gives Blue a couple of biscuits and they drive off to fill the car with gas, and then to Blue's favorite burger joint on Mission Street. Lily doesn't eat burgers, but one of the cooks recognizes Blue after all this time and gives him an extra-large burger with all the toppings.

BLUE

I am eating the best burger in the whole world! We sit outside while Lily feeds it to me piece by piece so I don't gobble it in two seconds flat. She says, "Slowly, Blue, so you taste each bite."

I even like the pickles and secret sauce. I think it is just mayonnaise with a bit of mustard, but it's the bomb! When it's gone, I lick Lily's hands and face because I love her.

• • • • • • •

As soon as Lily and Blue park Homer, she spots Mikey and Jewel and yells, "Hello!"

Jewel slowly stands from her lounge chair overlooking the river and waves to them. After hugs and pets, Jewel starts by saying, "Wow, you look good, Lily, and so do you, Blue."

They seem pretty much the same as before, still in love, still the mom and pop to the younger river people, still junkies, still dealing, and still without their daughter. Offering Lily a folding chair, Jewel shares the news that they purchased a used RV, which will be a safer home for much of the winter, and for when the cops roust the tent encampments.

After Lily and Blue left town, Jewel explains that the police did a huge bust and knocked down and ruined everyone's tents. People were devastated, especially the older folks. Jumping in, Mikey fast-talks about the previous tent community, how everyone scattered, and that a society of roving RVs is beginning to take hold. Lying against the back of his folding chair, he proclaims, "Tent camping near town is a scary, haphazard mess now, with so many fuckers sleeping in doorways, down highway ravines or under overpasses. We've done our part trying to help out, especially the young kids, but fuck it, it's overwhelming. The whole thing just pisses me off…"

Mikey is launching into one of his often-spouted and well-rehearsed monologues when Jewel gives him a pointed stare. He stops for a few moments.

Mikey and Jewel call themselves "sustainable junkies," meaning they keep their lives together, dealing drugs while cautioning their clients to be safe. Mikey whistles to Blue, who sidles over to him. "You know the story, don't you, Blue? Don't ever trust those mother-fuckers."

Blue sits next to Mikey as he continues trash-talking the people living up the river. Preferring the sunny, lower part of the San Lorenzo River closer to town, Mikey rants, "Those upriver fuckin' scumbags, those down-and-out thieves, they're useless. If I catch any of those motherfuckin' sick cockroach junkies trying to rip me off again, I'll blow their brains out."

Interrupting with her hand on his knee, Jewel calmly says, "They're depressed, their minds are fried, they need help but don't want it." Turning to Lily, Jewel explains, "We've been ripped off up there a couple of times. It's like scattered tent enclaves, quite down and out, and they operate like small tribal gangs. You can't blame them."

Mikey winks at Lily. "That's my Jewel, queen of the underdogs."

Thinking she'll probably never see Mikey and Jewel again, Lily wishes them the best and thanks them for being kind to her when she was living on the San Lorenzo.

Fuckin' Cool

The river is a small stream today. Tadpoles swim the marshes beneath the Water Street bridge unaware of two large egrets fishing nearby. Their snowy white-feathered necks bend and stretch, capturing the iridescence of light on water. Rich, verdant grasses line the wet edges in patches and clumps, concealing garbage, decay, and the snakes and frogs that find their purpose in survival.

Grumpy after her long work day, Jonnie thinks about the garbage and decay in her own life. "Fuck that shit," she says out loud, "I don't need to dwell on that past load of crap."

Using one of the plastic bags she carries with her, Jonnie picks up candy wrappers as she mumbles, "Some assholes think they can drop whatever they want along this river. Fucking morons, probably meth heads or junkies."

She knows what that's like and her heart goes out to them, but she hates people's trash behavior. As Jonnie stoops to pick up more garbage, she sees a thin, elegantly dressed man and his dog stop at a spot along the river. He wears a classic pinstripe gray suit with a white t-shirt and new red high-top tennis shoes. Removing his dog's rather bulky harness, he pulls a tennis ball from his pocket. Jonnie watches as the man stands and waits. His salt-and-pepper hair is pulled back in a tight ponytail. She hasn't seen him around town and wonders if he is a newbie to Santa Cruz.

Freed from her harness, the yellow lab runs down the path, sits, then barks two times. The ball leaves the man's hand and flies through the air in the direction of the dog. The lab catches the ball in her mouth and runs the ball back, where she places it precisely in the man's right hand. The dog runs off again, barks twice, and again the man throws the ball in the dog's direction and the dog returns it to him. This happens a number of times, after which, panting, the dog trots over to sit by the man. The man returns the ball to his pocket and replaces the harness around the dog's neck and shoulders. Petting the dog, he grabs the harness and the dog leads him along the trail. Realizing the man is blind, Jonnie slaps her leg and exclaims to herself, "Fuckin' cool!"

Since quitting drinking, meth, and blow three years ago, Jonnie sometimes calms herself after work by walking this somewhat-forgotten river. Carrying a trash bag, she picks up papers, used needles and condoms as she strolls along. Jonnie has had as hard a life as many of the dogs she cares for at the City Animal Shelter.

Up the path, Jonnie spots Lily and Blue lying on their brightly colored quilt in the sun. A couple of shiny black crows are bouncing nearby. As Jonnie gets closer, she sees Lily distractedly feeding peanuts to the crows. Lily looks up and waves. In a few strides, Jonnie flops down on their quilt. She gives Lily a howdy hand slap and wakes up Blue to give him what she calls "serious hug-a-dubs."

"It's good to see you, Jonnie," Lily says as she rubs Jonnie's freshly shaven head. She likes teasing her. "You look adorable."

Jonnie scowls and laughs. Among the myriad of tattoos and piercings on her body, she shows Lily and Blue the new turquoise-and-green dragon tattoo that crawls up her left shoulder to spew flying red finches and yellow parakeets across her chest and neck.

"That's the most poetic and beautiful tattoo I've ever seen," Lily compliments.

"Thanks, it took a long time to do and was just finished last month. It's from this totally surreal dream I had earlier this year and I had to ink it."

"So tell me, what's the dream?"

"Okay, there was this dragon. Well, the dream was kind of stupid, you know how dreams are. It was stuck in a cage and someone, maybe me, let it out."

Looking at the details of Jonnie's tattoo, Lily nods. "Go on."

"When the dragon was freed, it roared and instead of fire, all these birds flew out. The image got to me, so I looked up dragon symbolism. I learned that the dragon, a powerful mythological creature, can cause great harm but can also be noble and protective.

Two large crows sail in, landing on the grassy hill, their bossy voices asking for more peanuts. Lily gently tosses them a few handfuls.

Jonnie smiles. "In my dream, light-filled songbirds escaped from the dragon's mouth, took wing and flew to the heavens. I figure I am the dragon and the birds."

They both watch the crows take off to the trees nearby with beaks full of peanuts. Lily asks, "So what does that mean to you?"

"For me, it's a symbol that I'm done causing harm to myself. That I can now allow goodness and beauty." Jonnie finishes, "I know that sounds hokey, but you get it, don't you?"

Lily hugs her; she totally gets it. They both have traveled the long road.

BLUE

I wake up because someone is petting me. Jonnie! I stand and give her a big face lick as she chuckles this deep, rich laugh and hugs me. I love Jonnie, she is my favorite of our few friends in Santa Cruz. When Lily and I lived here, Jonnie saved my life. When I

got locked in a cage at the animal shelter, she fed and talked to me, and made sure I had a blanket to sleep on. She even gave me extra treats and told me she could tell I was a very smart and good dog.

I don't like to think about what happened back then. Life was very scary. Lily was drinking and doing too many drugs. She lost me more than a few times. Sometimes Lily didn't come back to Alice, our tent, so I would go looking for her. Cars almost ran over me and people yelled and threw rocks at me.

I was picked up by the dog police and put in a cage four times. The last time, Jonnie's boss came into my cage to make the decision. He wasn't as gentle as Jonnie. I had sores on my body, so when he touched me they hurt. I was very thin and scratched a lot because I had fleas. He looked closely at the scars on my neck from when I was a puppy. When I tried to wriggle away, he grabbed me. I was scared and gave him a warning growl.

Just then Jonnie came by my cage with food and I was excited to see her, but her boss said, "His time is up, he is not adoptable with all his scars and sores. It looks like he doesn't have a responsible owner, as he has been here too often and now looks worse than ever. Sorry, Jonnie, I know you like him and he obviously likes you, but he can't stay here much more than another day or two. We need his cage."

If Lily hadn't come to get me, I would have been taken to the back room that no dogs return from. Jonnie tracked down Lily and helped her pay the fines to get me out of the shelter. That's when

she and Lily became friends. Later Lily told me that Jonnie had saved my life and that she would forever be thankful to her. She thanked me for being such a good dog in the kennel.

After Lily got to know Jonnie better, she told me that Jonnie is like the United Nations all wrapped up in one person. Lily said that Jonnie is very wise and thoughtful. She said that sometimes Jonnie dresses like a he but is a she, and that Jonnie is a mix of at least three races. I love Jonnie because she loves dogs, especially me.

· · · · · · ·

Jonnie asks Lily what's happening in Los Angeles these days, and if she is seeing anyone. Lily tells her about volunteering at the shelter.

Jonnie shakes her head, "It's pretty heavy duty, isn't it? We couldn't do as much as we do without volunteers. I am proud of you, Lily, for stepping up like that. And what about you and any guys, have you seen Big Mac?"

Lily responds, "Yeah, I have."

"How's that going?"

"Pretty good, we're still just friends and going tortoise slow. Hopefully he's learning to trust me again like I am learning to trust myself. It's good 'cuz he's away a lot for work, which gives us space right now. It's a wait-and-see kind of thing."

The air is starting to chill. Lily unties her sweat-shirt from her waist and slips it on. "Blue's getting old, and it's time for me to find a regular job. I can never thank you enough for saving Blue's life."

"I don't need to be thanked every time we talk or write or see each other, Lily."

"Maybe not, but then again, maybe *I* need to."

Jonnie doesn't know what happened to Blue and Lily up on the Gualala, and Lily wants to keep it that way for the time being. Jonnie hears enough bad luck stories. One day Lily will tell her, just not now.

They chat a while longer and at their goodbyes, Jonnie says, "Be careful. I've heard that skinhead tweakers are coming into town from up north and will most likely camp along the lower river."

Lily thanks her. "You have my cell number."

"Yes, I do. Lily with a cell phone, now *that's* something!"

Wild Kingdom

Brilliant magenta pathways cross the golden bowl of setting sun as Lily nears Lighthouse Field. She is often dazzled by the beauty of this land and sky. It's the tilt and curve of the bay and the way the mountains drop quickly into this open mouth of Pacific saltwater. Alive and shifting, the land sits right on top of the active San Andreas Fault and can feel like the edge of the world.

Lily thinks of this part of California as a wild kingdom. Just the other day while hiking the dry golden grass fields up above town, she and Blue almost walked up on a female mountain lion sleeping soundly in the midday sun. They were so close that Lily could smell the cat's musky odor. Silently they crept backwards until they could hightail it out of there.

Testing the waters at Its Beach, Lily witnesses gray-headed pelicans gliding along the coast in flotillas of twenty or so at a time. Down at the sloughs and mud-flats, the pelicans are larger, with white-feathered heads. Blue cranes and white egrets wander the winter green of Lighthouse Field looking for frogs and rodents to devour. Lily's favorite time is the months when thousands of fluttering, burnt umber and terra-cotta monarch butterflies settle at Natural Bridges State Beach and Lighthouse Field.

Though the water is calm and seemingly quiet today, Lily knows the bay waters are alive with sea lions, otters, and a variety of perch, cod, and other fish. Whales travel north and south through the bay at different times of the year and seabirds flock by the thousands when sardines are running. Surrounded by tall cliffs and rock outcroppings, Its Beach slopes gently to touch the chilly teal water.

The first time they came to this particular beach, Blue paddled out to the distant jagged rock to investigate the sea lions preening and barking to each other. Lily grabbed his leash from atop their towel and swam as quickly as she could to the rock, where she practically had to drag Blue through the water back to shore. Once on dry land, she admonished, "Blue, you are never allowed to do that again. Though they bark, these creatures are not your tribe, they can hurt you!" Due to that potentially dangerous experience, Blue is only allowed to swim in the shallow water.

Lily and Blue have brought Patch, their quilt, to the beach to sit and watch the water and the sky as they eat their dinner of Trader Joe's goodies. The water shimmers liquid silver as the grapefruit-pink and gold sunset slides behind a narrow curtain of fog moving in quickly from the west. When done with dinner they head back to Homer to get ready for night. Blue jumps in the back of the car as Lily puts on her jacket and tells Blue she will be back in a minute. She closes the hatch-back, makes sure the windows are open a bit for Blue, and walks the short path to the bathroom.

Back at the car ten minutes later, she sees that Blue has crawled under his blankie to hide. He has done this occasionally ever since what happened on the Gualala River. Lily gently touches him and hums "The Rose," one of Blue's favorite songs. She sings, "I say love it is a flower…and you its only seed." Leaning over him, she tells him that he is a very good dog. He pokes his head out from under his blanket and gives her one of his worried looks.

"Okay, my prince of princes, my king of kings, I got it. We will call Norma and Big Mac and head home after a morning swim."

Early morning light enters the day with eastern pink skies almost as brilliant as the end of the day before. Lily and Blue crawl from their cozy car bed and stretch under one of the eucalyptus trees scattered through the park. Lily strips down to her bra and undies that pass as swim gear, grabs two towels, and she and Blue trot across the street, down the stairs, and race each other into the first welcoming wave. The salt water is chilly. Lily rises from her dive, ready to swim a few laps back and forth along a hidden line parallel to the beach.

Blue, wet from his quick splash into the water, shakes off and runs down the beach to romp and play with dog friends. Twenty minutes later, done with her swim, Lily dries off and lies on her towel to read a few pages of her paperback. Then she calls Blue and they walk up the beach to return to Homer. She reorganizes the back of the car and takes a quick potty break at the beach lavatory while Blue sniffs out the perfect tree trunk and lifts his leg, then waits patiently by the restroom door for Lily to emerge.

Cruising south on Highway 1, heading home east of The Angels, Lily whispers goodbye to Santa Cruz and their short but healing stay.

BLUE

With my head out the window, the sensation of my flapping ears, and the aromas of highway vegetation, car exhaust and the distant ocean, I feel a bit batty. It's a lot for a dog to take in, even a dog like me. Taking a break from all this open-window excitement, I partake in a well-deserved nap.

The smell of fried fish hits my nose and I wake with a start. I remember our meal at a little fry shack in Pismo Beach on our way to Santa Cruz and drool escapes from my jaw in drips and drabs. I hope we stop there again. Yup, Homer is heading to a parking place. Yum.

Lily orders shrimp salad for her and crunchy fried fish treats for me. We walk down to the beach and eat our lunch on the sand. Thinking I can snack

on more fried fish, I try to entice Lily into seconds by heading back up toward the fish shack when Lily calls out, "Blue, come catch me!"

We both start running down the gigantic beach. "Catch Me" is one of my favorite games because I am a much better player than Lily. She can never catch me and I always catch her. After our runaround, with both of us panting heavily, we walk back to Homer to continue our drive. I sleep most of the way to Norma's.

. . . .

Angelica

A warm breeze scrambles the leaves of the deep-purple plum tree as the doves flutter and coo in the afternoon sun. In full bloom, the roses release a gentle fragrance, lulling Lily into a dream state as she sprawls on the new papasan chair Norma got for the patio. Her turquoise notebook and pen are in her hands. Opening her journal, she writes:

> *Sometimes memory takes us places where we no longer live, like a foreign land once visited. All that's left are internal snapshots of place and time. The past is my teacher, because my life is now.*

Resting in the warmth of the afternoon, Lily reflects on her relationship with Mac. They have once again become close friends and she acknowledges she's in love with him, but is not in any hurry to make that known.

Months ago, she told him about the Gualala attack. Lily thought he would be shocked and supportive and was surprised when he expressed anger at her for putting herself in a dangerous situation. He questioned her need to be out in the wilderness alone, even with Blue, and they ended up arguing.

Lily remembers standing in the cottage kitchen, hotly debating, when she realized that Big Mac would never really get it. She flopped down on the sofa and said, "Mac, of course you don't understand, you're a man and have always been able to go anywhere you want. You do realize that, don't you? And now you're telling me that I shouldn't go where I want? Of course it's safer for men, and maybe most women wouldn't have done what I have, but I needed to go where I did. You're lucky; I bet that as a man, you have never wondered if any place is dangerous for you. And Mac, maybe because you have always been loved by your family, you've never needed to question your place in this world. You haven't needed to wander to try to find yourself."

At the end of their argument, Lily remembers saying, "And I don't need you to understand. I just hope one day you will accept what I need to do for myself."

Mac said he was sorry, that he understood, but of course he didn't. Then he went over to Blue and lay down on the floor and held him. "I'm so proud to know you, Blue, thank you for saving Lily."

He then sat next to Lily on the sofa. She remembers his sad eyes when he said, "Thank you for saving yourself."

Later that month, when Lily told him she was going back to "redo" her relationship with Santa Cruz, Mac was silent for awhile, then said, "I don't know how to do this."

"I know. But I'm taking a cell phone and will call often. I'm not doing this because I'm messed up. I'm doing it because I'm *not*. I need to make sure of that."

Now back from Santa Cruz and with journal and pen in hand, Lily clarifies her thoughts about the life-changing time on the Gualala River.

Getting clean and sober was my work to do on my own. I needed isolation to be able to hear myself and process my own thoughts. After what I did to Blue, I knew it was do or die for us, and I needed to do it my way.

Up on that isolated part of the Gualala River, the sounds of trees moving in the wind and birds chirping in those trees were healing, the fragrant flowers and wild plant scents were healing, the herons, hawks, frogs, crickets, dragonflies, insects, and little fish sharing the river with me were healing. The river play and swim chases with Blue, healing. Nightly campfires and clear view of the constellations, healing. The heat of the sun, the morning fog, the night moon shining on us, it was all healing…until a fucked up, sick human tried to take everything from me.

Lily shifts in the papasan chair and pets Blue's still-sleeping head. She looks at the roses and lavender and listens to the sounds of the birds and insects in the little patio garden, and continues writing her thoughts:

Some people, probably most, even Big Mac, think it's sweet when they see me feed the squirrels and crows, or when I say I was raised by the squirrels and birds of my childhood backyard. It's not sweet, it's true and incredibly sad that before Norma came into my life, I felt they were the only creatures who loved me. They were my kin.

My parents supplied me with food, clothes and lodging, but that didn't feel like love to me. No wonder I was so fucked up, but not now. I think the wilderness healed me and maybe the rape was just a horrible test. That's probably a bullshit thought, but I was only chosen because I was there. It's been hard for sure, but I am not devastated by what happened, maybe because I know he is dead. Dead. Dead. Dead. If that freak was still alive, I might feel different. I might live in fear that he would come find me. But that is not the case. Kill or be killed is a fucked-up option, but that is what it was.

As far as Big Mac's concern about my trip to Santa Cruz and my need to test myself, I understand. But I needed to do it and for me it worked, so Mac will have to learn that is just a part of who I am. I do love him and I feel more ready to be with him, but I can't give up myself to be with him, that is for sure. So we shall see what becomes of us.

Her reverie and writing done, Lily closes The Wonder and crawls from the papasan chair to check the time. Norma will be back soon, so Lily gets ready to go to the shelter to walk the dogs. It's her first time volunteering after being away this past week. She's looking forward to meeting the new intakes and finding out who adopted her favorite hound.

BLUE

I rest in the garden as Lily writes and absentmindedly feeds the squirrels. These fuzzy creatures zig this way and zag that way, all nervous and excited about the peanuts. I don't understand what all the hullabaloo is about, why don't they just come eat? I don't get all goofy when Lily hands *me* a shelled peanut to eat.

A party of birds flits around the bird feeder hanging from the lemon tree while a few doves march on the ground below. Two bossy pigeons push the smaller birds away from the feeder and acrobatically hang upside down to eat their fill. One little bird swoops down and lands on my back, he's a cute one. I think, *I could catch and eat this bird.* But of course I don't, and instead fall asleep. When Lily gets off the chair, I join her as she gets ready for her volunteer job, which means Norma will be home soon.

• • • • • • •

Norma picks up the phone on the third ring and right away Lily's words rush out. "Norma, my favorite dog is still at the shelter and she is now listed as 'unadoptable'.

She has become fearful in her cage and sits cowering in the corner. She hasn't been walked the whole time I was gone. She is scheduled to be euthanized tomorrow! Can you and Blue come right away to meet her, and if you both like her, can I bring her home?"

Norma grabs her car keys and Blue's leash and they drive to the shelter.

BLUE

When I enter the shelter, I want to walk right out again. It smells like the place I stayed in Santa Cruz and sounds like it too. Echoing sounds of dogs barking and whining, lots of people talking to each other or walking around. It's too noisy and I don't want to be here. Lily gives me a kiss as she takes my leash from Norma and leads us into a small, closed-door room where a tall, super-thin dog stands shaking in the corner. I look at her drooping, sad eyes and she turns her face to the side, letting me know that I am more important than she is. That's a good sign. I slowly walk to her as she slides down to the ground, then licks my lips, which is dog talk for "I know you are in charge."

I sniff her and let her sniff me. Lily tells us her name is Angelica and asks, "Blue, what do you think, can we bring Angelica home and help her to be happy? You will always be my Number One, but she needs us."

She and Norma whisper as they watch me continue to sniff Angelica. I like her smell, so I play-bow and she responds by wagging her tail. Though her ears are heavy, long flaps, I can see she is perking them. I start jumping left and right to see if I can get her to play. All of a sudden, she play-bows to me and we start jumping around each other, right there in that small room. I bump her side and she turns in a circle, it's fun.

I like her, she can come home with us, it might be nice to have a best dog friend. I go over to Lily and nudge her, then I pick up a tennis ball from the corner and put it in Angelica's mouth. Lily laughs and Norma comes and hugs me. Lily puts my leash on and puts a leash on Angelica, and we leave the room with Angelica still carrying the ball in her mouth. We wait at the front desk while Lily pays money and signs papers. I sit while Angie stands next to me. She doesn't know the rules, so I will need to teach her to sit whenever I do. After Lily is done, the three of us get in Homer and follow Norma's car home.

Angelica follows me everywhere and sleeps right next to me. I don't mind because she is very respectful and I like being her dog teacher. She is afraid of almost everything. When Norma or Lily open a door, she jumps backwards as though the door will hurt her, and when Norma gets out pots and pans, Angie hits the floor. She even peed right there in the kitchen a few times. Lily tells me that her peeing is called submissive peeing, that she is afraid she is going to be hit or hurt in some way. She says Angie has been abused by people for a couple of years, so it will take time for her to trust us.

When Big Mac first came over, Angie ran from him. Lily told Mac to sit on the floor with his back toward Angelica and not to look at her or raise his arms. When he did, Lily gave him cooked hot dog pieces to hold flat in his hand. Angie crawled toward Mac and he fed her a piece at a time. Of course I got lots of pieces too. Angelica watched Mac from a distance as Lily went back and forth between her and Mac, touching both of them. She says Angie will become more secure and braver the longer she is with us.

I try to share my stuffed toys with her but she has no idea what to do with them, so I show her. I toss them in the air and catch them, then put them on the floor right by her. She looks at them like they are space creatures. The only toy she likes is a tennis ball that she carries in her mouth.

• • • • • • •

Angelica reminds Norma of Dumplin' and Doolie, her hounds from years ago. She loves how gentle and sensitive hounds are, and knows they are often mistreated as they are stubborn. Norma thinks Angie is mostly bloodhound but maybe some coonhound as well. Her nose is to the ground wherever she goes and though she does not seem the smartest dog, she is smart enough to follow Blue everywhere and do what he does. Lily is a good trainer and Angie is starting to sit and lie down on command, and is becoming easier to walk on leash.

The Visit

The school year started a couple of weeks ago and Norma is back teaching her fifth graders. There's a new teacher at the school that Norma has been hanging out with at lunchtime. It appears to be one of those love-at-first-sight kind of things. Alexa is a couple of years younger and moved from Seattle to get away from the long, gray winters. Norma has not mentioned Alexa to Lily yet but plans to, soon.

It's late afternoon and Norma is sitting at her desk sorting through mail. There's a letter for Lily from New Mexico. She walks through the patio and places it in the cottage on the table so Lily will be sure to see it when she gets home. The dogs follow Norma from her house to Lily's cottage and back again. Tired in this late summer heat, Norma sits down to watch a movie. Blue climbs on the sofa next to her while Angie curls up on the dog bed.

Halfway through the movie, Lily comes running into the house, waving the letter from Ethan. "They want him to get rid of his animals. He's sick, and his parents want him to move in with them in Los Alamos."

Norma says, "Lily, slow down, what's happening?"

"Right, okay. ET wrote me that his parents are pressuring him to live with them. They want him to get rid of his goats, chickens, and Cleo. His letter doesn't sound like him. Why would they do that? Do you think he is really sick?"

Norma thinks for a second. "I think you need to know more. Come sit and breathe a few minutes, then call him from here."

Lily sits on the sofa to calm down, hugs Blue, goes over to hug Angie, then walks into the kitchen to call Ethan. After the initial how are you's, Norma hears Lily say, "Oh Ethan, I am so sorry. What do you want me to do? Okay, I have to ask Norma, but I am sure it will be okay. I will fly down in a couple of days."

Flopping on the sofa next to Norma, her lips quiver as she says, "ET has cancer. He says he's okay but he wants me to come down for a couple of days so we can talk face to face."

Two days later, Norma drives Lily to the airport. Ethan will pick her up in Albuquerque, and she will be back in four days. Norma will take care of the dogs while she is gone.

• • •

Driving up to the airport, ET sees Lily waiting on the curb. As soon as he stops, she hops in and gives him a quick hug. ET thinks she looks lovely, almost the same as she used to, but there is a difference in her. She seems quieter, older, as though her stance and her face have been enriched with the passage of time. He wonders if she recognized him or just his old truck.

ET has aged about ten years during this past year of being sick. No more long black ponytail, just a cap of salt and pepper, really mostly salt. Chemo didn't care, he was bald as can be for months, but luckily his hair has grown back. Placing his hand on Lily's, they silently pull away from the airport and head to the ranch.

As they drive along, Lily looks at Ethan. He's so beautiful, she had forgotten that. He has become very pale and thin and his eyes seem to have moved deep into his head, like he is looking inside. She can see he has been through a lot. When Ethan takes her hand in his, she remembers how much she enjoys being in his presence.

They don't say anything for most of the ride; it is enough to be near each other.

Nearing Tesuque, ET explains, "The ranch looks pretty much the same, a few more trees and planted garden areas and paths, but it's a bit in disrepair. I can't seem to keep up. The house has changed. Adrienne, my ex-girlfriend, had the walls painted and we bought new furniture."

"Where's Adrienne now?"

"She took off four months ago. It wasn't much fun for her, living with a sick boyfriend. She got a good job in finance in New York City."

ET says that his parents started getting on his case as soon as Adrienne left. "My mother calls me a million times a day and is driving me crazy with her worry. Dad, too." ET sighs, "I love them, but it's my life."

A bit overwhelmed by all this, Lily changes the subject and asks what he's reading but before he can answer, they are at his house.

"Let's go inside, I'll make us tea," Lily says as soon as they step out of the truck.

Trying to hide his exhaustion, Ethan says, "Lily, I'm glad you're here."

"Me too," she says, breathing in the high desert air she loves.

After giving ET a big hug, she grabs her backpack before he can and heads toward the house. Walking slowly, he shows her to the guest room, where Lily notices he has placed fresh flowers by the bed.

Ethan sits at the kitchen table as Lily fills the tea-kettle with water and sets it on the stove. From a shelf, she grabs a painted flowered teapot and two turquoise mugs she hasn't seen before. "These are pretty. You didn't make these, did you?"

"No, I still don't do that kind of pottery. Adrienne bought those at a fair when we lived together."

"I like them. Are you and Adrienne in touch? Would I like her?"

"I think so, she's fun, but she's not coming back. She loves living in New York, and we seem to call each other less and less."

They sit silently for a few minutes, waiting for the tea to steep. ET starts to say something but Lily interrupts, "Let's wait to talk about everything, we have plenty of time. Why don't you take your tea and go rest while I find Cleo and say hi to all the animals?"

As soon as she steps outside, Cleo the Cat runs up to her. Lily happily scoops her up and scratches behind her ears, saying, "Cleo, how are you? It's so good to see you."

Meowing loudly, Cleo follows Lily on her investigation of the ranch. Lily stops and kneels in front of her. "Cleo, are you asking about Blue, or are you telling me your worries with Ethan being sick this last year, poor little kitty? And just so you know, Blue is fine, and I am sure he misses you."

The enclosed raised-bed vegetable gardens are in disrepair; dead tomato plants, dry lettuce and shriveled beans fill the beds. Rotting plums and lemons lie on the ground for wasps to sip their fill. It's obvious that the goats have not been let out of the barn so they can help clean this area. Entering the barn, she smells the goat and chicken poop; flies are plentiful as she props the barn door open. As the animals wander out of the barn, Lily recognizes all of them, but realizes that Frank and Barbara, the goats, and Pearl and Jacqueline the chickens are missing. She picks up Gladys Chicken and gives her a little snuggle. Carrying her, Lily leads the animals to the vegetable and fruit tree area and closes the gate, placing Gladys in the tastiest spot as the other chickens and goats start foraging.

"Eat that up, little ones, while I go clean the barn."

Lily laughs as she watches them chomp and peck. Shaking her head at how much the animals are enjoying their feast, she grabs the work gloves and shovel and gets to cleaning up the barn. Halfway through, she finds herself whistling and chuckles at how much she enjoys this kind of physical work. When she's done, Lily sits on the bench outside, thinking. She is numb. ET needs help, and he is worse off than she anticipated. The heat of the sun soaks into her as she tries to absorb what's going on. Suddenly, like old friends, two large magpies sweep down and fly over her. She takes a close look and says aloud, "It can't be, but yes! Wow, you must be old by now."

When Lily lived here years ago, she named them Inspector This and That. They were so inquisitive and would inspect everything they found in great detail. Knowing magpies mate for life, Lily wonders how many babies they have had, and if they will still eat from her hand.

She sprinkles some of the chickens' sunflower seeds on the ground for them, goes back in the barn and changes the chickens' and the goats' water, then puts out fresh alfalfa for Simon and Linda, the remaining goats, and more poultry pellets, sunflower and other seeds for Gladys, Lucinda and Annette, the chickens. She's glad to see that ET still has everything well organized with plenty of food and treats for the animals, but wonders why he hasn't let them out to forage.

Finally, she carries a small bucket of dried worms with a few raisins to entice all the animals back into the barn for the night. They have done a good job with the vegetable beds, and Lily thinks another visit tomorrow will do the trick. After that, she'll let them wander the rest of the property to clear out the dead grasses.

Cleo silently follows Lily back to the house and to her room. As Lily unpacks, Cleo sniffs everything she pulls from her backpack then follows her into the kitchen, where Lily looks in the pantry and refrigerator to see what she can make for dinner.

"Come sit down, Lily, I have to talk with you," Ethan calls from the living room.

Lily wanders out of the kitchen. ET can tell that she doesn't want to discuss anything yet and is trying to sense what is going on without talking about it, but he pushes on. "I need to say this tonight so we can have a couple of good days together before you leave. I won't sleep well unless I can say what I need to."

Lily sits on the sofa with Ethan. "First, I want to say I'm sorry about Frank's and Barbara's passing, and also Pearl and Jacqueline. I hope they passed peacefully."

Ethan looks at his hands and says, "They did, but it's always hard. Barbara died in my arms. She was so old she could barely walk, but she came and found me at the end so I could hold her." With tears in his eyes, ET continues, "Frank died in his sleep, and Pearl and Jackie got sick. I nursed them a while but they were old and died almost at the same time."

Lily scoots next to ET and holds his hand. "I'm so sorry. It's a big loss, but they had a good life with you."

"That's true, they did." He gathers himself again, "So Lily, I need you to listen to me."

"Okay," Lily says, feeling a jumble of nerves in the pit of her stomach.

"I have a plan. I've been thinking about this for a long time, even before Adrienne left, as she was not an animal or ranch person. We got along in lots of ways but we were very different from each other, and I'm not too sure how much we really loved each other. Anyway, there's not much I can do about that now. What I want to talk with you about is this."

"I'm listening," Lily says, looking intently at him.

"It's a lot to ask and you can say no, if you like."

"Ethan, just tell me what you have been thinking about. You know me well enough that if I don't want to do something, I won't."

Same old Lily, ET thinks and chuckles out loud. "Okay, here goes. I'd like to give you the ranch. It is all paid for, so you would only have to pay the property taxes, insurance, and any upkeep you can't do. But I have some money that will help with that for a while." He rushes on, "I am hoping that you and Blue and your new dog Angelica can come and help me around the ranch as soon as you can. I can do some stuff myself but I tire easily, and as you can see, the animals are not getting what they need." He pauses to take a breath. "I know this is a lot to ask, and if you can't do it, I totally understand."

"Ethan, what are you talking about? I know you have been sick and I can see that you are tired, but you are healing. Of course I'll come help you with the animals and everything until you feel better, but you don't need to give me anything. You are my friend, you will always be my friend." Lily laughs, "I'll come help out until you get sick of me."

Lily starts to stand when ET grabs her hand. "Lily, I have to tell you…I really wish I didn't have to."

She sits back down.

"Look, for me, it has to be a two-way street. If you can help me, I want to help you. That's the only way. I know that you love the animals and will take good care of them. I don't want my animals going into a shelter. If you did want to sell the ranch, you can, because I know you would make sure you found good homes for all the animals. As it stands now, Javier will take Cleo but he has no room for the chickens or the goats. He works a lot and is not really a farm animal person. And my parents are pressuring me to go live with them in Los Alamos. I really don't want to do that."

Her face frozen, Lily looks straight at ET.

Another deep breath and ET goes for it. "The chemo didn't work. I have a rare form of leukemia and the doctors say they have done all they can. I went to every type of doctor and healer to make sure, and it's a closed case. As you can see, the chemo stole my hair and my energy, but it gave me some extra time. We don't know how much."

Lily looks ready to cry, her face gets red and her hands tremble, but instead she practically shouts, "What is this fucking shit? Ethan, what the fuck? Why didn't you tell me this before? You are not allowed to die, I just won't have it." More quietly, she adds, "Shit, you are too young, too special, you're such a good person, you are one of my only friends. I love you, you can't leave me."

Lily leans against Ethan, he puts his arm around her, and they cry. After a while Lily whispers, "Don't worry, Ethan, I'll take care of you and the animals, and we can discuss anything else later."

Ethan falls asleep on the sofa, which Lily notices is a new addition from when she was here last. Needing to block ET's announcement for a while, Lily focuses on the sofa. It's good looking, a modern beige sofa that kind of reminds her of her parent's sofa that she grew up with, but with colorful woven kilim pillows for interest.

Lily covers ET with a blanket, leaves him to sleep on the sofa, and wanders around the house. She can't allow herself to think that ET may die, it is too over-whelming. She notices that the bookshelves are still neatly ordered according to topic. There's a new painting hanging above the fireplace, magpies standing in the snow with the mountains and sky behind them. Lily looks at it a long time. It is a reminder of why she loves this New Mexican land. If Adrienne chose this, Lily thinks she really would like her. She'll ask ET at dinner.

One wall in the dining area is painted a deep rust, where a large pounded-tin mirror, almost like Norma's, hangs. As she wanders through all the bedrooms, she notices a new blue-striped area carpet in Ethan's bedroom. The wall behind his bed has been painted a lovely sky blue and there's a modern light wood dresser. A pretty floral carpet has replaced the older green one in the bedroom she's staying in, and it looks like the whole inside of the house has been painted white. Lily likes it.

The quilts she made are still on the beds, and she looks them over carefully. She had forgotten how intricate they are. There are new towels and bedding, and pots and pans in the kitchen. She thinks that she would never would have bought these things, but she can see what a difference all this makes. The house feels fresher and strangely happier than when she lived here.

While Ethan sleeps, Lily pulls a mattress, pillows and the farm quilt from her room into the living room and places them in front of the fireplace. She brings in wood from the woodpile and builds a fire. When Ethan wakes, he looks around and says, "This is nice. Are you okay? Is there anything you want to say?"

"No, I'm glad you told me now and I understand, so let's let that be for now."

Ethan and Lily sit on the mattress to eat their veggie, rice, and salad dinner. They talk about the easy things as they scratch the surface of catching up on each other's lives: books they are reading, ET's work, Blue, Angie, Norma, Lily's shelter volunteering. Lily asks about the magpie painting and he says that Adrienne took the abstract painting they bought together to New York with her, and he purchased this one last week at a small gallery in Taos. It's by a local artist and they can meet her one day if Lily wants. She tells him she loves the painting. He knew she would.

ET and Lily sleep all night in front of the fire with Cleo curled up and snoring between them. In the morning, Lily is clear what needs to be done. Ethan is still asleep as she creeps out of bed and goes to the other room to call Norma. A calm force takes control as she tells Norma what is going on. She will fly home in a couple of days, only to take off again in a day or two to drive back to ET's with Blue and Angelica.

Norma's voice cracks as she says, "I'm so sorry, Lily, give Ethan my love and let me know if I can help in any way."

"Thanks Norma, I will. I need to call Mac now."

Lily hangs up and calls Big Mac to tell him that Ethan is really sick and needs her help, and she hopes he understands. She will need to drive down a couple of days after getting home.

Mac responds, "I'm finished with this job and have a couple of weeks before the next one. If it's all right with you, I think it's time I meet this Ethan Tanaka. I would like to drive with you and the dogs."

Lily thinks, *This is why I love this man,* but she says out loud, "Mac Man, you are the absolute best, I would love that."

Late morning, on their way back from Santa Fe and the farmers market, Lily asks Ethan to stop at CVS to pick up food storage containers so she can prep meals for him to eat until she returns. He tells her that Javier and other friends will come and help while she is gone. She responds, "I want to cook for you anyway. When I come back, it will be good to see Javier again." Lily rolls down the window. "I love the high desert! It's the quality of the air, it's so powerful here in a way that's difficult to explain."

ET is reminded of when they first slept together under the stars out on the mesa. He knows exactly what she means. While he was in the midst of chemotherapy, he asked Adrienne to drive with him to parts of the mesa so he could rest under the expanse of sky. He'd bring two folding chaise lounges and blankets. It was so exquisite and healing for him, but Adrienne kept looking at her watch; she didn't understand. Looking forward to doing this with Lily, Ethan knows it's where they connect the most.

During their lunch of salad and grilled cheese sandwiches, Lily asks ET if he has been feeding Inspector This and That, the magpies, if that is why they are still here. He says he has, on and off, but he thinks they decided to make this their home. They eat whatever they want from the garden, and sometimes he sees them in the barn. As ET and Lily go out to take care of the animals and do a little work in the garden, ET happily notices that Cleo has more pep in her step and is following Lily or him wherever they go.

When ET goes inside to take a nap, Lily begins cooking one of her soups, remembering that Ethan used to tease her with the name "Wild Soup Woman." She decides to make a potato veggie soup with cheese rinds, cashews, and cumin. It's a bit odd but very hearty and ET has seconds. After dinner they watch the movie *The Switch*, a comedy with Jennifer Aniston and Jason Bateman. It's silly and it feels good for both of them to laugh. Lily keeps saying that Jason Bateman reminds her of Javier. ET realizes it's kind of true and that makes them laugh harder.

The next morning, feeling that the time is right, Lily asks, "Ethan, remember when you taught me to shoot?"

"Sure, that was fun. Hey, do you still have the gun?"

"I do. Remember how your dad told you, and you told me, to always shoot three times?"

Hearing something in her voice, Ethan stops and looks at Lily questioningly, "Yes?"

"Well, I needed to do that, and your instructions saved my life."

Ethan grabs her hand and walks them outside to a carved oak bench under an aspen tree, with Cleo following. As they sit, Lily slowly tells him everything. ET is silent.

"Please don't tell your parents, I'd rather they not know."

"Of course." Almost as a whisper, he says, "It's surprising how awful things can happen, and it's what we do with that experience that defines who we become."

Lily nods, knowing exactly what he means.

"I don't know what to say, Lily, other than I usually think of you as a bit fragile, but you are bad-ass heroic. Are you okay?"

"Yes, for some reason, I really am."

"I have to let this all sink in. Who else knows? Norma? Big Mac?"

"They both know, and I'll tell my friend Jonnie when the time feels right, you'll like her. But probably not others. I don't want people to characterize me by that event. I don't feel it defines me; it was just something that happened."

"You know, that gun can't be traced. It's a long story that Dad told me, but if bullets are found, they will not lead to the gun or to anyone who is living." Ethan switches position on the bench. "Has the body been found?"

"Yes, about two months ago, Norma read about it in the newspaper and showed me. It appears that a mountain lion found the body soon after we left, so it wasn't found for a long time and not much was left. They did find bullets, but nothing seems to have come of that. They tracked where he lived in Santa Rosa and connected him to the rape and murder of a few women. I think they are still investigating. Norma and I found four names of missing women from the area when we were looking, so I'm glad the police are now on it."

"Jesus," Ethan blurts out, "that is so awful." He grabs Lily and holds her tight.

"Those poor women. I have no remorse about killing that human, none. I don't even believe in capital punishment, but the truth of it is, I'm glad he's dead. It was either him, or me and Blue."

Quiet for a few moments, Ethan says, "Lily, you did the right thing. It does sound like that was the only way you could have survived; like you say, it was him or you, and much better him. And yes, you will have to live with it, but I would want you to do the same thing again in that situation. And you probably saved other women's lives by killing him."

He stops and absendmindedly combs his fingers through his hair. "I think you have become stronger, and maybe it's exactly because you needed to save yourself. I am proud of you, and Blue."

ET goes on, "It's not the same at all, but I felt assaulted by this cancer. After a long while, I stopped being so angry at my situation and became more understanding. I didn't give in, I just . . . *accepted* it, and decided that I want to live the way I want, with the time I have left. Even though my body is weaker, my spirit is stronger. And you, Lily, it's good your bad-ass self is alive and well."

Relieved that she has told him and he understands, she hugs him. "I don't ever want to be assaulted again to become stronger or changed for the better, so maybe your thinking is very fucked-up thinking, Mr. Ethan Tanaka, but I do happen to agree about our experiences and I think you are a very wise old man."

"What can I say, my child, my devoted Grasshopper? I'm going into the kitchen to get cookies, want some?"

"Sure do."

She waits on the bench until ET returns with a handful of peanut butter cookies. "Thanks for listening. I feel awful for the other women and their families, but I decided not to contact the police with what I know. Norma agrees. I don't really trust the legal system."

Ethan stands, "I agree, and thank you for telling me. I'm here if you want to talk more. But right now we'd better get gussied up for my parents. They'll be here soon, and it will be a trip as usual."

Becky and Howard

ET's parents arrive half an hour early, both dressed as though they play golf every day, though only Howard plays, and rarely. Howard wears plaid pants and a dark blue Izod shirt. He looks a lot like an older Ethan, but has an extrovert's smile and personality. Becky, his mom, looks quite conservative dressed in a white cotton Izod button-down long-sleeve shirt, a plaid knee-length skirt and small gold earrings that set off her short brown pixie cut.

Ethan feels the old judgments running in his head: that his mom "remodeled" his dad over the years from the hip, alternative Japanese American soulful rocker into a preppy engineer worried about retirement. He thinks maybe it's Los Alamos, a land of crazy engineers and money wannabes. But before he dives deeper into examining his parents and his childhood, he catches his train of thought with a silent admonition. *I am being way too harsh on them, they're good people and good parents.*

In truth, he knows they both love him and he loves them. Dad is easygoing and understands who Ethan is, and his mother certainly loves him though she has a hard time accepting the life he has chosen for himself. Marriage and children are what she wanted for Ethan. Because he has been successful as a ceramic artist, Becky is okay with that, but she has no understanding of why he would want animals and a ranch. Mostly she questions the women in his life, especially Lily.

His mom hops out of the car with flowers and a bag of Costco snacks and packaged food. Ethan thanks her and thinks, *Perfect, the goats will love this!* Lily glances at ET and holds back a giggle, knowing exactly what he is thinking. He gives her a quick wink.

Lily goes to both parents and gives them each a hug. "It's so good to see you, it's been a long time."

ET thinks, *Since when did she become Grace Kelly?*

Howard looks thoughtfully at Lily as Becky sweeps right past her and puts a hand on Ethan's hair. "Oh Ethan, it's so white, you used to have such beautiful hair."

Lily looks at ET and starts to say something, but doesn't.

"We want to take you into Santa Fe for dinner," Howard quickly offers. "Let's get going before it gets crowded."

It's five o'clock and Ethan doubts it will be crowded, but he knows they want to get on the road home before it gets too late.

"Let me turn off the tea water and lock the door. I'll be right back," Lily says over her shoulder as she walks towards the house.

At dinner, Ethan's parents ask Lily about Blue and about what she's doing. They know of ET's plans to have Lily come help him, in exchange for the ranch. His dad is tactfully trying to find out if Lily is up for the challenge. Becky is against the whole idea, as she wants Ethan to move in with them. Lily tells them a bit about Blue and Norma, then hesitates. Aware that Ethan's parents may not trust her, she wants to be clear with them as soon as possible. ET can tell she is done being cocktail-party nice and is going to say what she wants.

Glancing at ET, Lily starts. "Becky, Howard, I know you are worried about me coming back and taking care of Ethan, but I want you to know that I have changed." She goes on to state, "No more drugs or alcohol. Well, a little beer or wine sometimes, but no more running from myself." She looks at Ethan again, then his parents. "Ethan is one of the best people I know and one of my closest friends, so I am coming to take care of him, his house, and the animals. I don't want the ranch, but if that's the only way Ethan will do this, then I understand that too."

Taking her napkin from her lap and folding it on the table, she says, "I hope we get to know each other better and that you will learn to trust me for who I am now. But no matter what, I am going to help Ethan."

Ethan's dad takes Lily's hand. He can't make any words come out of his mouth. In the silence, Becky carefully wipes her eyes, then looks away. Howard pays the bill and they drop Ethan and Lily back at the ranch with quick hugs before heading home to Los Alamos.

When ET gets inside, he bursts out crying. "My poor parents, they are not supposed to outlive their only child."

Lily holds him as their tears fall. Ethan pulls himself together and stokes the fire, and they both collapse on the living room floor mattress to sleep next to Cleo and each other all night.

Road Trip

BLUE

Homer's getting packed again. That means another road trip, but this time Big Mac and Lily are loading the car together. Boxes of Lily's clothes, Magpie, and both of their backpacks. Hmm, not much food, I hope I have enough to eat. Now they are putting in Angie's bed, where's mine? Okay, here it comes, and Lily is putting it in the best place, phew, I'm still top dog. There's more being organized: Big Alice, jackets, and best of all, Angie's and my food and water bowls. I wonder where we are going, so soon after Lily came back home.

I smell something coming from the house. Norma and her friend Alexa are inside, I think I'll see what they're doing. I bound into the kitchen and lo and behold, they are making food. Norma gives me a slice of cheese and whispers in my ear, "Don't tell anyone."

Alexa laughs. She laughs a lot. I really like her, and it seems that Norma is sillier too. She's still the same Norma who loves everyone, but there is a lightness about her like a balloon lifting into the air.

As soon as Lily returned from her visit to New Mexico, Lily, Norma, and I sat on the sofa. After Norma listened to Lily tell about her time at the ranch and Ethan's health, and after Lily ran to get tissues, and after Norma and Lily cried a bit and I had to lick their faces to make them feel better, Norma told Lily and me that she had a new friend named Alexa. Well, that started a whole new, longer conversation and more tears, this time with happy faces and laughter. During all this time, Angelica slept. She sure misses out on the good stuff around here, sometimes even treats.

Later I hear Lily ask Norma if she wants to keep Angie with her. Though Norma likes her so much, Norma said Angie still needs her training with Lily and that she would be happier with me in New Mexico. Norma also said that she and Alexa have plans to take weekend trips and that Thanksgiving was not too far away. They both will fly to New Mexico to celebrate with us. I finally understand that we are going to see ET. I still remember him, though it's been a long time and so much has happened in my life since then. I remember those crazy goats, and that Cleo would sometimes sleep on my back. Big Mac is coming and then Norma will come later. I feel warm inside.

Lily whistles for me, but before I go out to the now fully packed car, Norma bends down and slips

me another piece of cheese and says, "Shh, this is our secret, I am sure going to miss you." Then Norma and Alexa hug me.

· · · · · · ·

After hugs all round, Big Mac, Lily, Blue and Angie hop in Homer to head for New Mexico. Norma calls out as she and Alexa wave, "We'll see you soon enough!"

With her head out the window, Lily shouts back, "Have fun, you two!"

In anticipation of this road trip with Big Mac and the doggies, Lily is almost giddy. No Google Maps for her, she pulls out her paper map to see the best directions to include Canyon de Chelly, a national park within the Navajo Nation. Anasazi ruins and petroglyphs from the ancient Pueblo People are preserved there. The canyon is the spiritual center of the Navajo Nation, more than one hundred and thirty acres with some Navajo families still living there. There is also a horse rental place and Lily is eager to ride horses through the canyon.

This is the first time Lily and Mac have traveled together and both are excited. Mac leaves the timing and side trips up to Lily, as he knows she is worried about ET. They take Highway 15 to the 40 and then haul ass to Flagstaff, as there's not much they will miss on the way. First to drive, Big Mac smiles as he clicks on music. "The rule of the road is that the driver controls the radio, so I don't want guff from any of you in the car, especially from Blue and Angelica."

Singing along with a Justin Timberlake pop song, Mac doesn't know any of the words so he sings a bunch of made-up gibberish. Practically in tears from laughing so hard, Lily teases, "Good luck making any money with *that* voice!"

Adding a deep mumbling gurgling sound, Mac laughs as he sings louder. Reaching over and disregarding Big Mac's rule, Lily turns the radio knob and finds a Motown station. The Four Tops'"I Can't Help Myself" is playing and Big Mac immediately joins in. He sounds pretty good, so Lily jumps in and sings along. Before the next song starts, Lily says, "I'm surprised you know all the words."

"My mom is a Motown fanatic. Whenever she cleaned house, which was often, she would blast this music. My brother and I had to help with the cleaning and Mom made it fun, or as fun as cleaning can be for a kid. I know a lot of Motown songs."

Lily remembers that when they lived together, he'd play loud music when they cleaned, but he usually let her pick the music.

They stop at a highway rest park for the dogs to pee and take a walk, and unwrap and eat Norma's lunch of green salad and cheese tortellini. Blue and Angie receive tasty bites of tortellini and dog treats, then they're all back in Homer and on the road. Their first overnight in Flagstaff they stay in a hotel, which is much easier than putting up the tent and unpacking all their gear. Lily and Mac freshen up while Blue and Angelica sniff every corner of the room.

"Pizza, everyone?" Mac questions.

Walking a couple of blocks from their hotel, they find a pizza place with an outdoor patio where they can bring the dogs. It's a chilly night though it's August, and Blue and Angie are wearing sweaters. Lily makes sure that Blue's body is kept warm, as he has become an old dog even though he is only middle aged according to the dog charts. Lily doesn't know Angie's age, so she makes sure Angie stays warm too.

At dinner, Lily tells Big Mac that Flagstaff is where she first played her guitar and sang on the street. It's clear by Mac's face that he doesn't want to talk about that time, right after Lily dumped him and she and Blue took off. He is quieter than usual for the remainder of the night, so the next morning as she's driving, Lily asks, "Is there something on your mind?"

Mac is slow to answer. "That was a really hard time for me, and I don't really want to talk about it."

"I don't know how many times I can say I'm sorry." Lily hates this discussion, if that's what this is. "I was fucked up, not ready, and I did what I needed to."

"Well, what else are you going to need to do? I just can't predict that."

"Mac, that's not fair, I've changed. But if you are going to hold onto believing that I could still just walk out on you, then we are going to have problems."

"I hate this discussion. I don't want to talk about this."

Lily sighs. "Okay, that's up to you. Hold on to old stuff all you want, but I think you do this to make me feel bad. And I think you like that."

"Okay, Lily, you really want me to talk about this? Well I *don't* like making you feel bad, but I don't think you feel that bad. You think saying you're sorry is enough. It's not. There's a next level to this shit that I don't think you want to look at." Mac is on a roll. "You have walked out on everyone, not just me but ET, Norma, even Blue. I get that you were abandoned as a child so you abandon those you love, but I need to know you are capable of being with me. I've chosen to give my time and my life to be with you again, and I want to know you are here."

Lily bangs one hand against the steering wheel. "I'm here, aren't I? This isn't fair, don't psychoanalyze me, and stop attacking me for what I did. I know what I did and you're right, I *have* walked out on everyone, I did do that. For Christ's sake, I almost killed Blue, what am I supposed to do with that?"

Lowering her voice as she realizes that she is yelling, she continues, "Maybe you don't trust that I really have changed. Well stay tuned, eventually you will see it's true. But if you decide you don't want to be with me, then that's the way it is. I can't do anything else than live my life now."

Somewhere during this argument, Lily turned off the road and stopped the car, and they both get out to walk around. Blue is visibly upset, so Lily lets him out of the car and hugs him and tells him everything is all right. Angie is asleep in the backseat.

Sitting by the side of the car, Lily's anger turns sideways and she starts crying. Mac is walking around, trying to shake off what just happened. His hurt is deeper than he realizes. If he is truthful with himself, he would admit that he may *not* be able to trust Lily again, but he doesn't want to see that part of himself. He'd rather be forgiving and kind than judgmental and unyielding.

Mac sits next to Lily and Blue. Lily has stopped crying and speaks first, "That was ugly of both of us. It seems like we have some issues to work out."

"We sure do. Also, I realize I am on edge about meeting ET. I hate to admit it but I'm feeling jealous. I went to my dark place and had a Mac attack."

Lily tries to smile. "Mac, you're right, saying I'm sorry is not enough. I've been really selfish, and all I can say is, let's give it time. We don't have to be anything, let's just *be*, and we'll see where our lives take us. I do love you, I know that, but that doesn't mean I understand how to love. One thing for sure, you don't have to be jealous of ET. I love him but like a brother, you'll see."

"I don't want to always worry that I am going to lose you. So I agree, let's just be and see what happens. I love you too."

They sit holding hands and staring at the dirt, and Blue stares at both of them until they look at him, at which point he stands and goes a few feet away to pee, as if to say, "If we are done with this, let's go.'"

Canyon de Chelly

Arriving just after noon at Canyon de Chelly, they check into a cheap but nice motel, take the dogs for a short walk and get them settled in the room, then walk to the horse stable.

A few horses are tied to a bar waiting for riders; they are both gentle and frisky. As Lily and Mac say hello and talk to the horses and move their hands over their backs, a guide who has been watching them comes over and asks, "When was the last time you each rode a horse?"

Lily says, "It's been a long time, but I love horses."

"Me too," agrees Mac.

John, the guide, responds, "Let's start slowly and we'll see how far we get."

Lily and Mac say, "Good idea!" at the same time, then look at each other and smile.

Pipaluk, Lily's horse, is short with little white stars sprinkled on her rump. John says her name means Little One. Mac is riding Aiyana, Endless Beauty, a bigger, taller, very handsome brown horse with a black mane and tail.

John is a Navajo man, slight of build, in fitted jeans, pressed shirt, cowboy boots and a hat. He's weathered, but everyone's face is weathered in this dry Southwest air. His eyes are bright and clear under his hat and his long ponytail is dark, streaked with white strands. A gold wedding band and beautiful turquoise ring adorn his hands. Lily is curious if he has a Navajo name, but doesn't ask.

She puts one boot in the stirrup and pulls herself up, swinging onto Pipaluk's back. Settling into the saddle, she rubs her face in Pipaluk's mane to smell her musky earth scent and breathes deeply. She smells of adventure, reminding Lily of when, as a young child, she would run naked in her backyard and roll on the ground to gather wet dirt and leaves on her body before splashing in her turtle-shaped plastic pool. She'd gallop around the yard pretending to be a horse for hours, encircling the few trees as she loudly sang to the birds and squirrels.

Holding the reins, Lily says a silent prayer of thanks as she looks out towards the expansive red rock valley. With the slight pressure of Lily's heels to her sides, Pipaluk carries her across dry earth that was once, thousands of years ago, the bottom of a vast ocean. Being a weekday, the canyon is not tourist crowded, so for today this land is Lily's and Mac's to behold.

After watching them a short while, John leads the horses at a gallop across the flat plains to a low river, which the horses walk carefully through to the other side. Traveling this ancient world of rock caves and petroglyphs, Lily is in awe. The combination of the dry air and light wind feels like an awakening. The longer they ride, the more alive both Mac and Lily feel. As their horses walk along the painted cliffs, Mac says to Lily, "This is mind blowing."

All Lily can do is smile. Maybe it's the blue of the sky contrasting the red rocks; maybe it's the silence, except for the breathing of the horses and the pounding of their hooves. Whatever it is, they feel the power of this place and are humbled.

Growing up on this land, John knows about animals and the natural world, but his understanding of people, especially the *Wasichu*, came with his own travels around America and the world. Age and past business experience taught John to be discerning, especially to whom he would gift his knowledge and love of this land. After years of running a successful business and raising his family, John returned to his beloved canyon and horses. Rarely did his riding clients feel respect and awe for this land, the home of his ancestors' spirits, or for the horses who carried them. Many tourists he met viewed the canyon as though it was Disneyland, talking loudly, taking photos, and barking questions at him like he was a cardboard stand-in for every indigenous person in America. John noticed that this young couple reveled in being here, the girl in particular. Chuckling as he watched her ride, he noted that she certainly was not a good rider but it didn't matter, as she lovingly clung to her horse as though they were one. Her spirit blended with the horse's spirit and with the valley. He could tell that Pipaluk enjoyed her rider.

It was clear to John that the young man loved the girl. He was a natural horseback rider with an innate understanding of balancing his body, as though he climbed ladders or worked on roofs. For a big guy, he was nimble. There was something else John felt about this guy, that he had a depth of heart, was solid and true. John liked these people and decided to treat them to a deeper experience of this place, his spiritual home.

Leading them down a ravine, John takes them to another part of the canyon where a hogan sits in the middle of a small flat plain. An old Navajo woman sits in the sun on a plastic lounge chair, knitting what looks to be a small baby blanket. The skin on her hands is as weathered and worn as the ancient rocks but the knitting needles in her hands fly through the yarn. She wears a traditional long, dark-blue velvet skirt with a man's plaid wool shirt and a heavy turquoise and silver necklace. John chats with her while Lily and Mac smile shyly and say hello. The elder nods her head in greeting.

Mac can't believe he's in front of a real hogan, and walks his horse closer to Lily's so he can hold her hand. He thinks, *I can't believe this is real, and not a movie.* The history of hundreds of years of Navajo life on this land is palpable.

Once the horses quietly walk past her home, John whistles loudly and they are off and running. Lily's face is caked with dust and her lips are as dry and cracked as the pounded clay soil. Her body bouncing with the movement of the horse's back, she tries to say something to Big Mac as she passes him, but her throat is so parched that only a slight squeak announces her joy. Lily's holding tight, loving every minute of this wild ride.

Back at the stables John quietly observes Mac and Lily dismount, pet, and thank Aiyana and Pipaluk. They walk to John, standing under a lone tree, to thank him profusely and tip him well. Mac takes his hand and says, "Thank you, John, that was magnificent. We will never forget this."

Lily whispers, "Pure magic."

John responds, "My pleasure. I don't normally do this, but I enjoyed riding with you and would like to gift you a little something, a bit of Navajo knowledge."

Lily looks at him as though he is a mystic teacher. She notices Mac also hanging on his every word. "Oh yes, please." Mac nods in agreement.

John's voice is gruff and has a finality to it. "Due to the world we live in, many of us do not use our Navajo names, sometimes only with our families. My name, Yiska, was given to me by my uncle at birth. It means 'Night Has Passed.'" Laughing, he says, "I was born just as the sun was rising. I think it was a very difficult night for my mother." He laughs again.

"What a beautiful name." Somehow Lily feels comfortable with John. "How lovely that names mean something special and particular to each person. It would be nice if our names had special meaning."

"If you are interested, I thought of Navajo names for both of you as I watched you ride through the canyon."

Stunned, they both nod.

"Lily, I would name you Yanaha. It means 'Brave One.'"

Lily's mouth falls open and she tries not to cry. Mac says, as he touches Lily's shoulder, "That is perfect, thank you, John. Very fitting, she is quite brave."

"And you, Mac, are like a rock. Your Navajo name would be Tse, which translates, 'Solid as the earth.'"

Mac shakes John's hand. "I'm not sure you know how much you've helped us. This has been a very special afternoon. Thank you again. I hope you have a good evening."

Lily hugs John and says, "Thank you. Really, thank you. I hope to see you again."

John casually responds, "You will."

Lily and Mac feel like they are floating on some kind of wisdom cloud as they walk to the motel. They take Blue and Angie for a good pee walk, feed them, then get a quick bite to eat at the nearest restaurant. Their day in the canyon stays tightly wrapped around them. Lily comments at dinner, "I think we are carrying the wonder with us."

Back at the hotel, she invites Mac to join her in the bathtub. Giggling at their clumsiness in the small tub, their naked bodies slippery in the soapy water, it becomes more comedy than romance. After what happened to Lily and Blue on the river, Mac has let Lily make all the decisions about when and how they would make love again.

One night a few weeks ago, while watching TV in the back cottage, Lily instigated it. Neither of them knew how she would react, but Lily said she was ready. With each move he made during their first lovemaking, Mac asked, "Is this okay? How about this?" He moved very slowly and Lily started laughing halfway through. Mac, not sure what was going on, asked, "You okay?"

Lily couldn't stop laughing. "I'm sorry, Mac, but all these questions . . ." She laughed so hard she almost fell off the bed.

Smiling, Mac commented, "Thanks a lot, my manhood's feeling deflated."

"It does look that way."

They both continued laughing, which led to roughhousing play, to reinflation, and then to a long, romantic lovemaking.

When they were done, Lily snuggled in and said, "I'm glad you are being so thoughtful, and I feel better about doing this than I thought I would. Go figure, life is so weird. I think we could go again, like we used to."

Mac responded, "Sounds good to me."

Lily had always been easy with her body and comfortable with sex; she enjoys it, especially with Mac, and that hadn't changed. As weeks went on and they made love more regularly, Lily told Mac that she didn't think she had any lasting sexual effects from the rape. Then she said, "Well, for now, anyway. Maybe I'm in denial, but it doesn't feel that way, so I think we should have all the sex we both want."

Dance Music

ET hears the car in the dirt driveway and comes out to meet them on the front porch. Lily jumps out of the car and runs to hug him. Blue runs after Lily and rubs against ET's body. His tail whirlybirds in circles to let ET know he remembers him.

ET puts his hand on Blue's back and says, "It's so good to see you, Blue."

He looks up as Angelica comes crawling out of the backseat, this goofy looking hound sniffing the ground as she slowly wanders over to lie down next to Blue. ET chuckles.

Mac comes around from the other side of the car and ET is surprised by his looks. In his mind he expected someone else, maybe someone less attractive. Carrying Lily's and his backpacks, Mac looks like a tall, handsome, burly woodsman. Before ET can think another thought,

Mac smiles and shakes his hand, saying, "So nice to finally meet you."

Lily steps back and practically sings out, "Ethan Tanaka, meet Martin Michaelson. Big Mac, meet ET!" Running back to the car, she unloads the dog beds, food, and other things they brought.

BLUE

I am happy being back at ET's and my tail seems to be wagging all the time. I am getting love from everyone, including Cleo, the goats, and even the chickens. There are only two goats and three chickens. Lily tells me that Old Frank the goat died, so did Barbara, and Jackie and Pearl were old and died too. ET shows us the little cemetery area where they are buried. I am not too sure what to make of this, but Cleo is still here and that's the best. I feel good in the dry air and don't have the aches or pains I have in The Angels. I can tell that ET is not well. He smells different than he used to, not how Lily smelled when she was doing too many drugs, but different. Still, he is kind and acts like he did when we all lived together, only he moves slower, like I do, so I like hanging out with him.

Cleo seems older too, but she recognizes me right away and we are best buddies again. Cleo is helping me train Angelica, who is not the most focused dog. Cleo and I need to be patient teachers. Angie gets distracted by the silliest things; for instance if she, Cleo, and I are going to see how the goats are doing out in the field and a fly buzzes by in the opposite direction, Angie follows the fly. I can imagine *eating* the fly, but just to follow it, now that is not how things are done around here. I have to go nudge her and then she will follow me again. Sometimes I have to body-slam her or grab her leg in my mouth to get her attention, that really wakes her up.

Lily is very busy. She cooks and cleans and feeds the animals, and sometimes ET or Big Mac help. This morning ET and Mac are working in the garden, planting root vegetables and trimming trees. Two days ago, ET showed Mac how his water recycling contraption works, then they fixed a broken fence so Angelica and the goats can't get through.

ET naps every day, and that is when Lily, Big Mac, Angelica, and I go adventure. Yesterday we went in Homer towards Taos and hiked a trail that Lily and I used to take. There are so many good smells as we travel over the mesa to end at the cliff's edge of the Rio Grande Gorge. We have to keep Angelica on a leash because of the steep drop-off at the edge, but she is getting better about staying close. Sometimes Lily gives me her leash and attaches it to my collar. I hold part of it in my mouth and Angie walks right next to me. She knows who's in charge.

Lily and Mac talk as they walk. I hear things about ET's health and plans for the next couple of days. I learn that in a couple of weeks, Mac is going to fly back to The Angels for work. I sure am going to miss him. Lily and Mac hold hands for much of the hike. At the edge of the mesa, as we look at the river far below, they kiss a couple of times. We all sit on a

bench right there and look at the view, then we start the long walk back to Homer. We drink fresh water that Lily pours in a bowl and Angie and I fall asleep in the backseat.

· · · · · · ·

The sky is enormous and the air crystal clear as they walk northwest down the Rift Valley Trail. The Sangre de Cristo Mountains wrap the mesa north to south. Black Mountain and Agua Fria Peak are in the distance but Lily doesn't know which is which, and thinks she will ask ET later. Reaching the dramatic edge of the steep ravine, they overlook the snaking Rio Grande, which has carved through these plains for centuries. This is Lily's favorite hike and she tells Mac that she never gets tired of it. Lily asks Mac to make a wish, and she does too. Keeping their wishes secret, they look at each other and know they are in love and can do this next part of their lives, together and apart.

After the hike, they go up to Taos so Lily can give Mac a quick tour. They purchase fresh flour tortillas to have with soup tonight and handmade corn tamales for tomorrow's lunch. The dogs are conked out as they drive back to ET's. Arriving at dusk, they stand in the yard watching the sky turn a collage of pinks, golden oranges, and silvery blues.

ET and Mac are trying to bond. From the kitchen window, Lily watches them talk in the garden and makes salad for lunch. Everyone has been shy and proper around each other, with most of the talk centering on Blue and Angie, or Cleo, or the goats and chickens, or the garden and house. Nobody knows where the emotional boundaries are, other than Ethan and Lily are great friends and Mac and Lily are a couple, but that understanding doesn't answer everything. Mac and Lily sleep together at night in Lily's room, then in the morning Lily goes in to lounge and talk with ET in his bed. They have a very close bond that Lily doesn't want to lose, especially now. She's trying not to be the person in the middle—but she is, and all three feel the tension.

That night after dinner, ET lights a fire as Lily strums a bit on Magpie, then she puts Magpie away and they all sit silently.

"I'm feeling kind of uptight," Big Mac says as he stands and walks around the living room. "I think we have been walking on eggshells, trying to be polite."

"I feel that too," ET agrees.

"Me too. I think we're trying to act normal, but I don't know what is normal in this situation," Lily says.

ET adds, "I think we have to just be ourselves, as this is a major change in all our lives. But we need to figure out how to unwind some of this tension."

Mac suggests, "Let's blow it out, act stupid and dance, okay? ET, what albums do you have? Any Marvin Gaye?"

ET responds, "Great idea, I have just the thing." He smiles and stacks a pile of records on his old record player. "Let's wait for Marvin, he'll be second."

First comes mariachi music, which entices them to jump around hootin' and hollerin'. Next comes Marvin, the long version of "Got to Give it Up."

As ET swirls and jives around the living and dining rooms, he yells, "This has to be the best dance song ever!"

The music is blasting and the dogs are dancing too, running around from one person to the next. The humans are twirling and stomping, lost in their own thoughts but sharing this abandon with each other. ET is the first to plop down on the sofa, Lily follows, then Mac falls to the floor, quite drama-queen style. They are all out of breath and smiling.

The dancing breaks the ice a bit and they feel more relaxed. The next day, Ethan places three dime-store folding chaise lounges and a few blankets in the back of his truck. Too tired to drive, he gives Big Mac directions to way out on the mesa where there is nothing. They lounge for hours watching the sky change, the clouds performing like actors on a huge sky stage. Similar to a long meditation, all three sit in silence, knowing they're connected to each other in this unknowable story.

At one point, Mac looks at Lily and tears are running down her face, then notices Ethan tearing up too. Mac breathes deeply, thinking, *This is going to be powerful.*

That night Lily puts candles everywhere as Mac makes a mushroom omelet and spinach salad. For dessert they eat a whole chocolate cake they bought in Taos and top it off with a bottle of Malbec. Ethan looks at Lily when the wine comes out and she winks at him, knowing she can have a glass of wine and not want more.

Mac has been reading about the ongoing drought in New Mexico and asks ET about it. They get into another conversation about the gray water recycling system ET put in a couple of years ago, which leads into talk about the ranch's well water and septic systems, then the roof solar panels. ET was working toward being totally off the grid when he got sick. Mac is fascinated and asks all kinds of questions as Lily listens in. She's interested but loses focus when they get into the technical and construction discussions.

Eventually she changes the subject to taking a trip to Canyon de Chelly together, if possible before Thanksgiving. ET likes the idea and tells about his time in the canyon. "It may sound weird, but Canyon de Chelly has always felt like my spiritual home. I have been there a number of times. Years ago Javier and I spent three days on horseback, riding around as much of the park as allowed. I know it sounds awful as it is Navajo sacred land, but we snuck in one night and slept outside under the stars."

Lily smiles at him. "The sneaking is probably awful and disrespectful, but I understand. We were there for just one afternoon and I think both Mac and I felt a deep connection there, too." Lily tells ET about the Navajo names John bestowed on them and wonders what name he would give ET.

"I don't think I'll have time to go at Thanksgiving

before everyone gets here. What do you think about going after New Year's?" Mac asks.

That sounds good to the three of them. They decide to have a big Thanksgiving feast with Ethan's parents, Javier and his girlfriend Cindy, and Norma and Alexa. Lily will invite Jonnie and her new girlfriend. Two days later, Mac leaves for his job in LA.

Small Bowls, Mugs, and Plates

The summer/fall crop is ending and the winter potatoes and root veggies have been planted. Lily feeds the chickens and goats while ET checks the garden to pick any beans, greens, tomatoes, and corn that may be left. Today it is ET's turn to feed Blue, Angie, and Cleo. Lily and ET are getting used to living together without Big Mac. Later in the day, returning from the last farmers market of the season, Lily goes out to look at ET's studio while he takes a nap. It appears he hasn't done any clay work for months.

Over tea, Lily inquires, "What's going on with your clay studio?"

"What do you mean?" Lily gives him a look, to which he responds, "I can't work on my large water vessels or pots anymore, they're too heavy."

"Why don't you create small pieces like bowls, mugs or plates?"

ET becomes huffy. "I don't do that, I make large urns and fountains."

"Well, it looks like things have changed, but you are still an artist and a craftsman, and should be working on whatever art you can. At least that's what I think."

"Well, go ahead and think what you want."

"Well yourself, Mr. Tanaka! I used to do drugs and get drunk all the time, that's what I did, until I couldn't do that anymore. I had to find a new way to be, I had to figure out who I am and what I can do now. If I can do that, I think you might want to consider what kind of ceramic artist you are right now."

"Whoa, Lily, I get your point."

Ethan whistles and Blue, Angie, and Cleo follow him outside into the garden. "Lily sure can crack the whip," ET says aloud as he walks away. "What's this shit about figuring out what kind of artist I can be now?"

He calls Javier and asks what he thinks. Javier is on Lily's side. ET moans, "This being sick and dying really sucks, and now my best friends think they can order me around."

"Yup," Javier replies, "get used to it."

ET hangs up, takes a deep breath and sits quietly for a few minutes. He has been working on meditating.

Years ago, he used to meditate all the time, but he's rusty and his meditation is constantly interrupted by thoughts. It's still a good, quiet time, and he is getting better at it day by day. Now that he's off chemo and starting to feel better, ET misses having his hands in clay. He decides to go out to the studio to tidy up.

BLUE

The mornings here are chilly, so Lily dresses me in either a blue snowflake doggie sweater or a raspberry-colored fleece. I can't decide which one looks better on me. I think both must look great because when Lily takes me into town to market or the coffee shop, everyone smiles and says how cute I look. What can I say, I'm a handsome dog.

Returning from today's excursion to the market, I jog over to ET's studio, where he's spending lots of time these days. He's placed two soft, squishy dog beds in his studio for me and Angie. ET talks on and off while he works. "Don't tell Lily about what I'm doing, Blue. I want it to be a surprise, and I have a lot more to do on this new collection. You know, Blue, artists work alone for a reason. They need time to understand what is needed and what isn't. I know you are good at keeping secrets and not interrupting my process. You are an excellent studio pal."

I shake my head in agreement. Angie wanders in for a second, then goes back to the main house to lie around with Cleo. I think Angie is part cat. She's acting more and more like one, rubbing her body along the sides of walls and stretching when Cleo does, not that I mind. I'm just saying I have a lot to think about these days.

A couple of afternoons a week, Lily volunteers at the animal shelter. She tells me that shelter animals become easier to adopt the more attention they get, and she likes some of the people she has met. Lily is learning new training skills at the shelter, so every morning after breakfast she does fifteen minutes of training with Angelica. She walks her on a leash and practices her sits, stays, and handshakes. I look on with disdain as Angelica is not very good at any of it.

Lily tells me, "Blue, not every dog is like you, you are very special. Angie is learning basic dog behavior skills and that may be all she can learn. We don't love her any less. Just like people, dogs are gifted in different ways. Angie is soft and gentle and loving, she is my beautiful princess, *mi bella princesa*. And YOU, my wonderful Blue, my dearest boy, are my prince of princes, my king of kings."

I love it when she says that.

. . . .

Between Heaven and Earth

Time is flying by. It's an early winter and snow covers the ground much of the time. ET's parents visit every Sunday. Sometimes they go out to dinner, but usually they all cook at home. Javier drops by often to hang out, chop wood for the fire, and help Lily with other things around the house.

Ethan directs his limited energy to creating organically shaped bowls and vases. He hand-builds them, then cuts holes along parts of the rims to weave in heavy wire, from which he hangs clay shapes. His new series has become his creative obsession and conveys the idea of floating between heaven and earth. It's frustrating work, trying to balance the added shapes, and he has trashed quite a few pieces.

As he likes to say to Blue and himself, "No matter the rejects, the artistry is hidden between the concept and the design."

Blue has become ET's steady partner in the studio. It seems that Blue has decided that it is his job to watch over ET like a nanny watches over a baby. Throughout the day, like two peas in a pod, Cleo and Angie wander into the studio to check on Blue and ET. They sniff, look around, then meander back to the house. ET won't allow Lily in his studio, so when lunch is ready, she calls across the yard for him to come inside.

Slowly stirring his bowl of vegetable soup, ET dips a chunk of French bread into it, trying to finish what has been put in front of him. He is not very hungry these days but he knows the thought and care Lily puts into each meal, so he does his best.

When he's done, Lily shows him the envelope she just received containing her first letter from Father, ever. Now in his seventies, he wants a connection; he's retired, with a new woman, and wants to come visit. Lily doesn't know if she wants to see him. She remembers how manipulative he was, calling for her to take care of him when was in the hospital for two days. She and ET discuss what his visit might be like and decide that Lily needs more time to think about it before she says yes or no.

That night ET and Lily are at their favorite place on the mesa, sitting on folding chaises, staring upward. The air is so clear that the stars appear to hang low enough to touch if they raise their arms. As they hold hands, they imagine the sky soaking into their bodies.

Big Mac is done with his job and arrives back at the ranch a few days before Thanksgiving. ET is glad to see him and drags Mac into his studio to show him what he's been working on. It is going to be a surprise, especially for Lily. Mac is impressed and a bit in awe of ET's talents. Asking Mac to help him build a long dining table, ET says he wants to seat at least twelve people for Thanksgiving dinner and his existing table is too small. He wants to move the furniture out of the living room and put this bigger table in front of the fireplace. Behind the chicken coop is a stack of old barn wood ET wants to use. They go out to the woodpile and pick out interesting boards.

Lily, Mac and Blue take a hike in the afternoon, leaving ET, Angie and Cleo sleeping on the mattress in front of the fireplace. As they trudge up the steep mountain trail, Lily tells Mac that she and ET get along really well, but are so similar that they get into a very quiet and serious way of living. She understands now why their relationship didn't work years ago. Then she laughs, adding, "Not counting all my pot smoking and drinking." She tells Mac, "I think ET and I do best when you or Javier or some third person are around to un-nerd us a bit and lighten us up."

She stops walking. "I love Ethan very much and I want to stay here, but I hope you will come stay as often as you can. I miss you. I am realizing that I like myself best when I am with you."

"I really like myself when I am with you too, Lily. You said before that I was the fun for you; well, you are the magic for me."

"Mac, you are much more than the fun for me."

On this silent path, under the immense cerulean sky, surrounded by snow-dusted pristine white mountain peaks, they kiss.

• • •

It's early evening when Ethan shows Mac ways of constructing furniture that Mac has never seen. Mac thought ET would leave construction of the table to him, but they are doing it together, under ET's direction. Using no nails, in the traditional Japanese way of notching wood together, Mac watches as ET shows him step by step. It is a very precise skill, each piece of wood carefully cut and sanded to fit exactly so. Mac is trained in set design, which is quick and temporary. Ethan is an artist, patient and methodical, a master builder. They plan to get started on the table early in the morning. If it's to be finished by Thanksgiving Day, they don't have much time.

They hear Lily yell, "Boys, dinner is ready!" then her laugh. At the kitchen table, she says, "It looks like you two are having fun. Will you tell me what you are doing?"

"No way," ET smiles, "and no peeking! Just two more days and then you'll see."

"And don't look at me, I am just the helper," Mac chips in.

Lily twinkles as she brings the platter of avocado

sandwiches to the table. She can see that ET and Big Mac are enjoying each other.

• • •

Bunches of flowers are at the entry, in the bathroom, and scattered around the house, which has been cleaned top to bottom. Like two mother hens fussing, Norma and Alexa join Lily in the kitchen to cook. By dinnertime, an elaborate vegetarian feast is ready. Becky and Howard bring the cooked turkey, free range and organic as ET requested, and extra folding chairs. Javier and Cindy bring pumpkin pie and a chocolate dessert.

With ET's help, Big Mac has emptied the living room of almost all furniture. They have become secret buddies these last days and are acting like two kids, whispering and pointing and having way too much fun keeping Lily in the dark. Angie and Blue furtively lick any final bits of treats they can find on the kitchen floor. Norma has always snuck food to Blue, and now between her and Alexa, the dogs eat a feast before the real feast begins.

There is a bit of spice bickering between the new couple; Norma wants her Mexican spices on the potatoes and Alexa, Italian seasoning, their separate taste traditions for the holidays. Norma wins, and they both chuckle at their first minor spat.

Showered and dressed for the Thanksgiving celebration, Lily enters the living room, excited to see what has been secretly planned. ET and Mac are standing with controlled faces, trying to block her view of a long table in front of the fireplace. She looks toward the kitchen, where everyone else is standing. ET and Mac step aside, and Lily goes over for a closer look.

The first thing she notices are colorful stars, flowers, leaf petals, and other little shapes dancing high above the table in the flickering candlelight. As she gets closer, she sees small, variously textured vessels with cuts and holes in them so the candles inside beam light in every direction and onto the shapes floating and dangling above. Thin and thick, beautifully sculpted wires bend and fold to hold shapes that hang and balance. Running down the center of the table are ten of these vessels, with floating objects of all sizes and shapes. Each art piece looks to symbolize something. One is a tree, with branches, twigs and leaves suspended high above. Another is egg shaped, with birds flying every which way and feathers floating down from wings.

Each sculpture is a different story, and Lily is struck silent by their beauty. She tries to exclaim but chokes as tears well up. She goes and hugs ET. It's too much to take in. Lily goes back to the table and realizes that it, too, is hand-built of various pieces of colored barn wood, intricately assembled. She looks at Mac and ET and points at each of them, and they both laugh.

Mac says, "ET is the master, I just followed directions."

ET chimes in, "Mac had some great ideas and is a good carpenter. And you, Lily, are the one who challenged me to do clay again. I didn't think I could work small. This collection is because of you. Thank you. It's called Between Heaven and Earth."

Lily still can't talk without tearing up, so she looks at everything more carefully. The sculptures are so light and delicately balanced, fanciful but serious, each one either climbing to the heavens or holding tight to the earth. The table is earthy but also refined. Lily floats through the rest of the day and evening. Not wanting to say it out loud, she whispers to herself, "This is the best day of my life. I never want it to end."

• • •

On the plane heading home, Alexa turns to Norma. "That was lovely, Norma, thank you for letting me come with you."

"Are you kidding? I really needed you by my side. Did you see how gaunt Ethan is? My heart is breaking for him and his parents. It wasn't easy watching Becky's and Howard's facial expressions throughout the night. Their sadness must be devastating, and they hide their feelings as much as they can. And Lily? I don't know how she will handle this."

"She is taking excellent care of Ethan," Alexa remarks, taking Norma's hand.

"Lily is happy living there, that's obvious. I hope her and Mac's relationship lasts this time, I adore him. He is good to her and good for her."

From her carry-on case, Norma unwraps the sculpture ET made and gifted to her. It is a bowl shaped like two women's hands and tiny hearts with wings fly above, delicate and hopeful. Norma and Alexa silently read ET's card:

> Dear Norma, Thank you for being Lily's anchor and mentor. I have learned how fragile love and life can be. I hope you and Alexa have found the love you both want.

Norma tears up and fidgets in her seat. Alexa puts her hand on Norma's knee.

BLUE

My tummy feels full all the time from eating so much delicious food during the long Thanksgiving weekend. Lily laughs and tells me that I look like a little porker pig. I don't know exactly what that means, but as she says it, she rubs my large tummy.

"Time for a walk, my plumpy prince. Let's wake Angie and go out for a pre-breakfast stroll. I'll see if Mac's out of the shower."

We return to a special breakfast that Ethan cooked for all of us. Angie and I get scrambled eggs and turkey sausages mixed with our kibble. Cleo gets eggs, and Lily, Mac and ET have coffee, fresh-squeezed orange juice, French toast with maple syrup, and mixed fruit salad. Afterward we all go outside to do the chores and say hi to the chickens and goats. Angie and I go to our different hiding places to relieve ourselves. I see Lily running toward me with my snowflake sweater and Angie's sweater in her hands. As she dresses us, she says, "Look how

white the sky is, and the air is very crisp. I need to keep you both warm, you little monkey dogs."

· · · · · · ·

Lily doesn't care much about celebrating her twenty-seventh birthday. It always seems too close to Christmas, and she doesn't like to make a big deal out of it. Paying no attention to what Lily has said about doing nothing, Mac and ET take her into Santa Fe for a restaurant dinner. They order a cake with candles and sing "Happy Birthday" right there in the restaurant as all the other diners join in. Totally embarrassed by this attention, Lily admits to herself that she does feel special, but most of all she loves being with ET and Big Mac.

Snow flurries start on Christmas Eve for a true white Christmas. Norma and Alexa flew in two days before, and on Christmas Day, Jonnie and her new girlfriend, Heather, arrive an hour before Becky, Howard, Javier and Cindy. The last to arrive, just as people are sitting down to dinner, is Lily's father, who is staying at a hotel in Santa Fe. Lily decided to invite him with the assurance that Norma, ET, and Mac would make sure all went well.

Father seems much older than Lily remembers. However, as she watches him, she also remembers that he mostly talks about himself to whoever will listen. After dinner he shamelessly flirts with Cindy, who handles the intrusion but rolls her eyes at Javier as she walks away. As Father moves over to talk to Lily, Ethan and Mac watch, and Lily can't help busting out in a big smile as she sees them staring at her just like Blue does. Of course Father thinks the smile is for him. True to form, throughout the evening he doesn't lift a finger to help.

Later, when Mac asks how she thought it went, Lily says, "Seeing him once every few years will be more than fine, and maybe just for lunch in town. No matter what he wants, it's not my job to make him feel that he was a good father when he wasn't."

Presents are opened after Father leaves. Becky and Howard went all out and ordered handmade sweaters for ET, Big Mac and Lily, which fit perfectly. Lily's gifts to the humans are colorful handmade Mexican style cut-out cards. She purchased silly moose antler headbands for Blue, Angie and Cleo. Wearing them only a few seconds, Angie and Cleo shake them off and lie down by the fire. Blue, of course, loves the attention, and hops around and moonwalks quite stiffly as everyone watches and claps. Holding him afterwards, Lily tells him, "Old Mr. Hambone, I do love you."

Over the next few days, Jonnie and Heather bicker. Heather is demanding, and Jonnie, who has quite a crush, takes it. Thankfully for everyone else, the two of them leave every day to explore the surrounding areas. When they leave for the airport, Jonnie says apologetically, "This high desert is so beautiful, I will come back alone. It's not for Heather, she thinks it's barren and ugly."

Hugging goodbye, Lily says, "It's true, it *is* barren, but I think that's part of what I love here."

"Me too," Jonnie agrees. "Maybe people like us

find beauty in this forlorn landscape."

"What do you mean, people like us?"

"People who have experienced a kind of broken-ness. Or maybe it's being dreamers; people like us who look at the sky at night and see and feel more than the stars."

"Jonnie, this is *so* why I love you. You can take a normal conversation and make it deep and meaningful. Come back soon. I miss our talks and just hanging out with you. We do have a special bond."

"Yes, we do."

• • •

The day after Christmas, Alexa, Norma and Lily investigate Santa Fe galleries and shops. After a few hours they have had enough and stop at a cafe to eat. As they chat, Lily expresses her worries about ET's health. Sipping her tea, Norma offers, "We don't know what or when anything will happen. Trust your instincts, Lily, but don't forget to take time to care for yourself as well. I hate to say this, but there is no preparing for loss. I know when my mother was dying, I tried to take each day and treasure being with her, in whatever way I could. It helped."

"I will try. I am surrounded by thoughtful people, some of that wisdom should rub off on me."

Alexa takes Lily's hand and says, "I think you are wiser than you know."

And What About Time?

By mid-January, life on the ranch settles down as the silence of deepest winter takes hold. Darkness arrives early this time of year, and Ethan is thankful for the blanket of snow that muffles sound and keeps everyone quietly inside by the fire. He likes having Lily to himself while Mac is in Albuquerque working on a TV series.

It's morning, and Lily walks into ET's room and flops down on the end of the bed. He is sitting propped up on pillows, the blue quilt tucked around him, staring out the window. His gaunt face is pale in the filtered winter light as he watches the bare cottonwood trees standing still in the frozen air.

"What are you thinking about?" Lily asks.

"Oh, hi," ET says as he turns his head to face Lily.

"I was just remembering how I thought it was going to be difficult having you, me, and Big Mac all living here together. I thought I would be jealous and it would be weird, but it isn't at all. I was thinking that he is the glue that holds us together, and we both need him here with us." He stops for a second, "I think you are my real-life sister and that is why we met those years ago."

Lily lies beside him, pulls up a pillow, and puts his arm over her shoulder. "I totally agree."

They talk a long time about how it's so hard to live in the moment. The discussion morphs this way and that until they wonder whether a tree is aware of its existence.

Lily asks, "Do you think us humans love our lives more than a tree loves its life, or more than a chicken, a lizard, or a dog loves its life?"

ET and Lily's bodies snuggle in close. Their physicality is intuitive, a molecular understanding as though they have been babies, children, teenagers, adults, and old people together. It's as though they have known each other through many lives. It is the rare comfort of the deeply trusted.

ET ponders, "What about a tree's attachment to the earth, to the soil, knowing its place? And what about the chickens, goats, Cleo, Blue or Angie, do they feel more attached to their place on earth than I do?"

Trying to come to terms with what his own connection to life means, ET knows that he loves his life, that he has been lucky to have always known that. But now he has no idea what it will feel like when he is forced to let go of this life. Lily says that she is just learning what it means to love her life; even though she has always felt connected to the animals and the earth, she is newly discovering her place in the world.

Lily gets off the bed and brings back two warm cups of honey tea. As she snuggles back under his arm, Ethan wonders out loud, "And what about time? How does time affect each of us? Does it matter that my life is ending early? Does that mean I have loved life less or more?"

"I don't know . . . ET?"

"Yes?"

"Why do you think we are alive?"

ET thinks for a while, then says, "Of course I don't really know, but if pressed, I think we're alive to *experience* our living, no matter what our lives are or have been. I think it's like when I am working on an art piece: If it turns out beautiful, that is only a bonus; it's in the act of creating and honoring that process, that's where the meaning is. Does that make sense?

"Yes, it does.""

Lily and ET lie silently together.

BLUE

When Lily and ET go up to the mesa to watch the sky, I am the only dog who gets to go. The first time

this happened, Lily told me, "Blue, I've learned from Angelica that some dogs need watching while other dogs, like you, know to watch their person. I can bring you anywhere, my little prince, because you like to stay close. Angie lets her nose distract her, and if I am not watching her she could get lost, so sometimes I leave her home with Cleo."

Lily brings a raised-sling dog bed and wraps a warm fleece blanket around me as I crawl up and circle around to get comfortable. ET and Lily have folding chaises and quilts. My bed is right next to Lily and ET is on the other side of her. The three of us watch the clouds move over the sky, perched just above the snow-covered ground. Lily has hot chocolate in a thermos and water and biscuits for me. We stay until the air is dark and the stars hang way up high. They don't talk much; sometimes they whisper. I try to be quiet and watch the sky, but I usually end up falling asleep.

Big Mac is gone a lot, but when he's home, he and I go out behind the big house near the bare aspen tree, where he works on a small indoor platform he is building for ET. The ceiling and sides of the structure are made of old glass windows. The floor and side posts are wood to hold the structure in place. Big Mac tells me he wants to create the illusion of a floating room. He envisions a peaceful place where ET can take naps and see the land and sky in every direction while he is warmly wrapped in quilts, relaxing comfortably on a king-sized mattress.

Mac interrupts our work to say, "Shit!" He is stuck on part of the build. He grabs a pencil that rests behind his ear and scribbles numbers and lines on a pad of paper, then crumples the paper and shoves it in his pocket. "Come on, Blue, let's go commune with the goats, I'm getting nowhere."

I trot along beside him to talk with the goats.

. . . .

Three Days

It's the beginning of February and the snow has stopped temporarily. Looking online, Big Mac sees that it's going to be sunny for the next week. He, Lily and ET sit at the dining table to devise a plan. Nothing is said out loud but they all know ET is getting weaker; his night sweats are worse and he's losing weight. If they are going to Canyon de Chelly, they need to go soon.

ET is clear. "We need three days: one to get there, as the drive to Chinle, Arizona is long; day two to be there; and the last afternoon we'll drive back home."

Mac contacts his work and takes the time off. ET calls his parents and asks them to come stay to take care of Cleo and the farm animals. They often stayed at the house when ET had chemo, so it won't be any different this time. Blue and Angie will go to Canyon de Chelly with them. Both will be fine in the motel room while the humans are horseback riding. Javier wants to come, and offers to drive his Ford Explorer. Mac calls John at the horse stables to see if they can rent a truck or something to get out into the valley, as ET may not be able to ride that far.

Mac starts to remind John who he is when John stops him, "I know who you are. Who is coming?" He says he will have something ready for ET to travel in if he gets tired. *It's like he knew we'd call,* Mac thinks as he hangs up.

It's off season, so reserving two rooms for two nights at a motel is easy. The night before they leave, Ethan's parents come to stay. They bring books to read and bags of food. His dad prepares dinner for everyone, an inventive creation of maple syrup-soaked grilled cheese logs with scrambled eggs in small bowls on the side of the plate, so the eggs don't mix with the syrup. At the table, Lily and Mac look questioningly at the food, at each other, then at ET. Before anyone can comment, Howard proclaims, "This is Ethan's favorite meal."

"Yeah, Dad, it was my favorite when I was five." Everyone laughs and digs in, as it's delicious. Howard smiles.

After dinner, Becky pulls a family album from one of her bags. They are mostly photos of young Ethan on family vacations and at school, and his first few ceramic shows. They tell stories and chuckle at ET's childhood bowl haircut, his teenage hairdos and punk-ass clothing. Beyond everyone's smile, a deep sadness drifts through the air, latching onto everything. Mac stands and says, "We have an early start tomorrow, I'm ready for bed." Everyone says good night, and Becky and Howard go to the kitchen to clean up.

• • •

After the long drive and a good night's sleep at the motel, with the dogs fed and walked, ET, Mac, Javier and Lily eat a rather greasy breakfast at the local diner. Then they meet up with John, who is standing under the cottonwood trees at the horse stables.

"Good morning, Yiska," Lily says, giving him a hug.

John's eyes crinkle into a smile. As Mac shakes his hand, he introduces ET and Javier.

John asks Javier, "You have a bit of blood in you, don't you?"

Javier looks surprised. "Some Cherokee from my mom's side, no one ever notices."

John says, "Hmm," and rubs his horse under his mane. "I saddled three horses for you and set up this wheeled cart that my horse is used to pulling. Ethan, it looks like you can handle riding a horse for a while, so Lily will start in the cart. Are you all right with that?" He looks from Lily to Ethan. "When you get tired, you can change places."

In the cart, they see a mattress, pillows and two boldly colored striped blankets. ET is smiling ear to ear as he pets a medium-sized palomino. "Let's get going," she says as she crawls into the open side of the cart.

"Ethan, your horse's name is Mai, which means Bright Flower. She will be a bit frisky. I hope you can handle her."

Already on Mai's back, Ethan says, "It's been a while and I'm not that strong these days, but I've ridden horses my whole life." He leans over and runs one hand down Mai's neck.

"Mac, you are on Aiyana again." Mac beams.

"Your horse's name is Tulip," John says to Javier, "a retired thoroughbred racehorse. She's a great runner. Can you handle her?"

Javier responds, "I'm a fair rider."

John responds with his typical, "Hmmm." He watches as Javier mounts Tulip, then jumps on his own horse's back.

As John pulls off with the cart, Lily asks, "John, what's your horse's name? We didn't ask last time."

John turns in the saddle and winks at Lily. "Johns-Boy, as he's all mine."

The temperature hangs just below fifty degrees and everyone is dressed warmly. The air is crystal clear and the hard earth valley is frosted with patches of snow. Riding in the cart as it jogs along, Lily lies back, surveying the ancient cave dwellings, petroglyphs, and sparkling azure sky as they meander across this primitive plain. Intermittently she observes the three guys on their horses as they walk, trot, and gallop.

John leads the way down to the river, chuckling now and then when he hears oohing and aahing about the ancient sandstone cliff dwellings and rock formations. ET is in heaven and can't stop smiling. He bends down to whisper in Mai's ear. She looks back at him each time she starts to gallop, as if to ask, "Are you ready?"

By the river, John stops and says, "It's been an hour. How are you doing, ET?"

ET asks, "Lily, are you okay for a while longer?"

"Sure, let me know when you want to switch."

"Okay." ET sighs, "I want to wait til I'm exhausted."

John dismounts JohnsBoy and grabs a bag from the cart to offer bottles of water to everyone. ET chugs his and John gives him another.

A little later, ET rides up beside John and says, "I'm done. It's Lily's turn to ride Mai."

Everyone looks at ET, who is white as snow. Both Javier and Big Mac jump off their horses to help him off Mai and into the cart. Lily hands him more water and wraps him in one of the blankets. Leaning back against the pillows, ET rests and Lily climbs on Mai with some help from Big Mac. Then they are off to another part of the canyon.

ET feels like a king, being pulled comfortably behind JohnsBoy. He watches the mountains and cloud formations, then finds himself waking up as they head into the stables.

"Hi, sleepyhead," Lily shouts as she gallops by, her hair blown back and her face windburn pink.

At the stable, Lily slides off Mai's back and kisses her neck, saying, "Thank you" into her ear, and Javier and Big Mac walk around to get their legs working again. Javier supports ET to help him out of the cart. Ethan is a bit wobbly; he overdid it, but loved every minute.

"Bring the horses into the barn and take off their saddles and blankets, you'll see where they go. Ethan, you come sit on this bench and wait for us." With the horses and saddles taken care of, John queries, "Are you coming back tomorrow?"

"Yes," they all answer at the same time.

"Ethan, will you be able to ride Mai for a short while? I want to take you to a place the cart cannot go. We will be riding less than an hour, round trip."

"I can do that."

Lily whispers to John, "It may be too much to ask, but I'm going to anyway."

Smiling, John replies, "Go ahead and ask, Brave One."

She laughs at John's response, as she did have to muster her courage to ask. "Have you thought of Navajo names for Ethan and Javier?"

Without answering, John walks around the bench to face ET and Javier. "Lily asked me to give you Navajo names. Javier, you should be given a Cherokee name to honor your heritage, as your ancestors fought with their lives and survived the Trail of Tears for you to exist."

Embarrassed by this attention, Javier says, "I would appreciate that."

"I don't know many Cherokee names, but I think this one may fit: Degataga. It means Standing Together."

Javier puts his arm around Ethan's shoulders and says, "I like it. Thank you."

"Ethan, your Navajo name is obvious. It's Shilah, which means brother." John walks away, saying, "I'll see you tomorrow. Get a good night's sleep."

The Ceremony

When they arrive at the stables early in the morning, John is prepared. Each has the same horse, with Lily riding Pipaluk. John has saddlebags on JohnsBoy, with one of the blankets from yesterday rolled against the back of his saddle. He leads them at a leisurely pace across a small creek, then along a narrow canyon path between two tall cliffs. The horses clip-clop softly on the red dirt until the canyon walls open into a large, flat plain surrounded by rock faces. John tells them to ride around until he calls for them.

The four take off galloping, with Javier riding next to ET and Lily and Mac going a different direction to meet again in the middle. The air is so cold their breath forms clouds as they exchange words.

John calls them over and asks them to tie the horses, reins loose, to a metal ring attached to a single wood post dug into the ground nearby. He then directs them to stand at the outer edge of a circle he has drawn in the red earth. In the middle he has built a small fire. He takes a few sprigs of sage from the saddlebag, lights them in the fire, and circles each person including himself with the purifying smoke, mumbling words under his breath. Placing the folded blanket at a point on the circle, he asks Ethan to sit there, and motions the rest of them to sit around the circle.

John pulls a short stick adorned with feathers and leather ties from his bag and points in each direction. Looking up to the sky, he says, "According to Navajo tradition, *Yah*, the sky, the roof of the world, is held up by the four sacred mountain peaks that surround this land: Hesperus to the north, Mount Taylor to the south, Blanca Peak to the east, and to the west, the San Francisco Peaks. In blessing this circle of friends, we are here to hold up Ethan, Shilah, our brother, as he gets ready to pass from this life to the next." After a pause, he asks, "Ethan, is there anything you would like to say or do?"

The light shifts and the air seems to change weight as ET sits quietly for a moment, then spits on his hands and grabs the dusty red dirt beside him, spreading it on his cheeks and forehead. "More than anywhere, I feel a part of this high desert land. My hands have been creating art with this red clay my whole life," he says in a cracking voice.

Lily goes to ET and places more red dirt on his chin, neck, and the tops of his hands. ET takes off his jacket, sweater and shirt for his friends to mark the dry rock powder on his chest, back and arms. For the first time, they all see the large, flat, purple blood clots on his thin, pale chest and back, a prescient reminder of the disease's progression.

Lily quietly whisper-sings a couple lines from "Misty Roses." A lament of love lost, it's the first song ET mentioned to her years ago, when they first met.

> You look to me like misty roses, too soft to
> touch, but too lovely to leave alone.
> You look to me like love forever, too good
> to last, but too lovely not to try.

Tears run down everyone's cheeks as they place their hands on ET. One by one, they rub a bit of the red dirt on their own foreheads, cheeks and chins. John watches and puts more wood on the fire. After helping ET put his shirt, sweater, and jacket back on, the friends return to their places in the circle. ET seems in a trance. They all do.

Motioning for them to hold hands, John yells up to *Yah* with deep, mournful cries. The cliffs echo back and when they all join their voices to his, it becomes the complaint of all the living of this world. Eventually their howls soften and are stilled.

"Every person on this sacred earth," John starts, "is given life. It is within the nature of each person to choose how they live that life. Even the man in chains has some choice."

Mac looks at Lily, and Javier and ET hold hands as John continues.

"The indigenous peoples believe that all of life is connected in Spirit, which includes all humans, animals, trees, the land, everything, even the stars." A shift in air ruffles the flames and John places a few sticks on the fire. "This sense of Spirit allows us to inhabit our own eternal place. By eternal place, I mean knowing your own connection to life, your private native country. To say it another way, the you that is the True You. Seek the place where you belong, as this will help to create an attitude of acceptance and understanding. When you do that, you will be free. Free to live, free to die."

John pauses, then looks directly at ET. "Ethan, Shilah, your time in this world will be short. You are a gentle and kind being, endowed with great spirit and creativity. Your friends are here to support you, so live as true to yourself as you can. Each day, celebrate your aliveness. When the time comes, you will be ready to let go of all you have known to allow your Spirit to fly free."

Tears streaming, body shaking, ET takes in every word. John throws dirt on the fire and scatters the remaining charred sticks under the dirt to make sure no sparks are left. As they untie the horses from the post, John notices that each one hugs and pats their horse, as they also had been part of this blessing and need thanking. Javier and Mac help ET mount Mai.

John leads them out of the canyon and across the creek, then asks, "Do you know your way back?" They nod. "Okay, don't be long."

The four look at each other. Ethan turns his horse to the north, loosely wraps his reins around the saddle horn, and gallops off in front of them. His arms are spread wide like a man on a cross, surrendering himself to life in the middle of this holy valley, his ride of a lifetime, his joy of being alive.

Another Layer of Letting Go

During the morning ride and canyon ritual, everything that could have been said and done, has been. Lily packs the car while Javier and Mac take Blue and Angie for a walk before the long drive home. The dogs sleep in the way back with the bags and ET rests in the backseat with his head on a pillow on Lily's lap. No one speaks.

Upon their return home, a new easiness takes over. ET has an air of understanding woven around him. He spends much time meditating and deepening his understanding of what "letting go" means. Some days, followed by Cleo, Blue, Angie, the goats and chickens, he wanders his land, touching the trees and large planter boxes, now barren in winter. His hands trace the edges of fences and the sides of his house, barn and studio. Memories of his first years, creating each path and each planted garden shape, invade his thoughts. ET remembers all the work that went into designing and building the barn and his studio. He chuckles at his own heightened drama when something didn't go the way he planned and he had to redo it, his artist's passionate and critical nature getting the best of him.

Over the years, Ethan placed each bench or sitting area to catch the sun at different times of the year. He built most of the outdoor furniture or bought it at the flea market. During these walks, he stops to sit and thank each bench, chair and table. The large boulders he has collected and hauled into specific places in the garden are honored.

And finally, his beloved studio is scoured inch by inch, thoroughly cleaned and organized. This is his temple, the cornerstone and symbol of his life of creativity. The bags of clay, hand tools, ceramic wheel and huge kiln have been extensions of ET's being, inseparable from the blood flowing through his veins. It is in his studio where he allows his deepest sorrow of leaving this world. It is also where he is the most thankful for being able to live this life of expression, turning lumps of earthen clay into meaningful objects of beauty.

Big Mac is on high octane all week: he chops a quarter cord of wood, thoroughly cleans the goat and chicken barn, and vacuums and mops the entire house. He wants to get things done before he has to go back to work, and he is dedicated to finishing the little structure out back in time for ET to enjoy it.

Cindy and Javier come over the next afternoon for dinner and to stay the night. Lily has her typical pot of veggie soup cooking and makes bread pudding with caramel sauce. After dinner they put on their nightly dance music. Since returning from their time in the canyon, ET wants to have dance time after dinner most nights. First up tonight are the Four Tops. Everyone sings as they dance, "I can't help myself, I love you and nobody else." The Grateful Dead are next, and ET and Javier get in a dancing groove all their own as the others sway and swing around the house. No longer constrained to the living room, their dancing becomes a whole-house kind of jig.

For the last song of the night, Mac plays Joan Armatrading's "Me, Myself and I." Cindy gets all excited, saying her mom listened to Joan all the time when she was young and took her to one of her concerts when she was eight. She and Mac know all the words and twirl and stamp their feet as they sing.

Every night the music varies; Mac's favorites are Marvin Gaye and Joe Cocker. When ET was young, he was into heavy metal but he is their jazz person now, mostly old school John Coltrane and Miles Davis, and he introduces Lily and Mac to Pharoah Sanders and Milt Jackson. Lily's well-known additions to the mix are Bob Dylan, Nina Simone and Amy Winehouse. ET purchases African tribal music and Native American chants, which become dance and vocal favorites.

After the dancing, an often nightly ritual has become going outside and yelling, not at each other but up at the dark sky and at the many stars staring down on them. ET and Lily love this and scream their hearts out, while Mac joins in sometimes. On this particular night with Javier and Cindy there, they all yell in unison a few times, then burst out laughing and go inside for hot chocolate.

BLUE

It's cold today, snow covers every bit of ground and clings like white fluffy cotton to the tree branches. Lily dresses me and Angie in our warmest sweaters and we walk around the property together. Out on the land behind ET's studio, we play chase. After a few rounds of "Make Angie Run Fast," Lily whoops and hollers and falls on the ground, waving her arms and legs back and forth in the snow. Angie and I wriggle and prance around her.

Lily stands and laughs, "Look, we made a dog paw snow angel." She yells toward the studio, "ET, do you want visitors?"

ET shouts back, "Sure, come on in."

We traipse over to say hi and as Lily opens the door, I see two Cleos—one walking around, and one sitting very still with her head staring forward.

Lily exclaims, "Wow, that is beautiful, it's so Cleo, so queen-like!"

ET replies, "I thought of Bubastis, the ancient Egyptian city where cats were sacred. They were guardians of the temples and protected the dead. Do you like it?"

"Ethan, I love it. You captured Cleo's essence. She's become a fierce guardian angel for you."

"Thank you. That is what I was hoping."

I don't know what they are talking about but I lean against ET for some attention. He scratches behind my ears while I think about the two Cleos.

Lily interrupts my thoughts, "Lunch, anyone?"

I dog-mumble, "Hell yeah, let's go."

• • • • • • •

When Mac returns after his work in The Angels, Ethan, Lily, and Mac go out to lunch in Santa Fe. It's a treat to window shop and wander the wintery streets. At lunch, Mac asks ET and Lily if his best friend Tay and his parents can come visit for a few days. ET says, "Sure, I'd love to meet them."

Lily is nervous to meet his parents but Mac says not to worry. "They will love you both, and the ranch."

His parents rent a condo in Santa Fe and Tay stays at the ranch. Mac invites them to a special lunch, along with Becky, Howard, Javier and Cindy. The house looks well cared for and ET, Mac, Tay and Lily have made quiche, vegetable rice salad and pumpkin soup, with brownies for dessert.

Excited for his parents to meet everyone, Mac is acting like a happy kid. He walks his parents around the ranch, including the little resting house he is building for ET, which is almost finished. No one else has seen the inside yet; curtains on the glass walls hide it. Greg, Mac's dad, carries Lucinda, his new chicken friend, as he investigates every part of the ranch, and he includes Blue, Cleo and Angie in each conversation he has with the chicken. Greg seems interested in everything, and it's obvious he doesn't worry about what others think of his goofiness. Mac's mom, Pam, laughs a lot and has the same openness as Mac. Greg and Pam spend a long time with Ethan in his studio and truly appreciate his work. Like Mac said, they're easy.

Spending a few days hanging out with Tay and Mac's parents, adventuring around Santa Fe, Taos, and Chimayo, Lily sees how close and accepting they are with each other. She can tell that his parents adore Mac and that they also like her. Lily likes being around both of them as well, and tells them they are welcome at the ranch anytime. Remembering what Norma said long ago, "We don't pick our parents, it's just luck of the draw." Lily knows Mac got lucky.

It's mid-March, and ET feels himself slipping and sliding into the close of his life. Drifting through thoughts and in and out of sleep, much of the day he rests on the floating bed in the glass structure Big Mac has finished. A couple of days ago Mac quietly celebrated the unveiling of his gift to ET with the three of them, and of course Blue, Cleo and Angie. He made tea and muffins, which he carried out to the structure. The floating bed is a platform with cables hidden by painted wooden shapes that conjure the mountain peaks of the north, south, east, and west holding up Yah, the sky. Warmed with electric heat, the room remains cozy even in the winter chill. The mattress is topped with an enchanting indigo velvet night sky quilt that Lily made for his fortieth birthday, which will be in mid-April. She gives it to him when the glass house is finished, as they all feel ET will not make it to his fortieth. ET loves it, and with help climbs onto the bed. That night he and Lily sleep in this tiny glass house together. The transparent ceiling and walls make ET feel as if he is suspended between heaven and earth.

Javier comes to stay as many nights as possible. ET can't handle dancing anymore, and one night says he wants to play a song by Leonard Cohen, that if he ever got married this was the song he wanted to play. He now knows it's a song about his friends, his family, the animals, his art, the trees, the soil, the stars, everything.

> Dance me to your beauty
> with a burning violin
> Dance me to the panic
> 'til I'm gathered safely in
> Lift me like an olive branch
> and be my homeward dove
> Dance me to the end of love

Singing softly along, Mac, Lily, and Javier hold ET as they slow dance together.

Since returning from Canyon de Chelly, ET feels John's words as though they were carved into his soul, "…inhabit the you that is the True You…when it is time, you will be ready to allow your Spirit to fly free." Thoughts of gratitude well up as he thinks of his family and friends tending to his needs. As an artist, he has spent years alone, working singularly, digging into the recesses of his being to create something true and meaningful. ET feels fortunate to have done the work he loves, and to have made his living doing so.

From what ET has read, he will be on morphine soon to mellow the pain that has crept into his joints, muscles and bones. His breathing has become labored and the only exercise he can manage is walking between the glass abode—which he has named the Temple of Heaven and Earth—his studio, and the house. It surely was a sad goodbye when he realized last week that he no longer had the energy to create objects of beauty and meaning with his hands. His artist's life, over.

One morning in early April, ET wakes to Cleo walking ever so gently on his body. He will miss Cleo, but she is now loved by Lily and Mac. Cleo's behavior toward ET has changed. She looks at him differently, like an all-seeing doctor, monk, or spirit guide in a cat's body.

Lily and Blue lead the goats and chickens into ET's glass temple for a visit, and he chuckles as he watches this silly parade of his beloved animals. Continuing his gentle laugher, ET tells Lily that he couldn't have done this without her. She says she knows. It seems like years ago that he wrote to see if she could come take care of him, but it has only been a little more than six months. ET falls asleep thinking of his little collective of family and friends, animal and human, drawn together for his benefit to help him face what is imminent.

. . .

Today is Ethan's fortieth birthday. Ten days ago, on April 6th, under an expansive blue sky dotted with billowing white clouds, Ethan died on the mesa he loved. Surrounded by his parents, Javier, Cindy, Mac, Blue, Angie, Cleo and Lily, Ethan let go.

A few days before he died, needing more and more morphine to ease the pain, ET asked Lily to bring him to his favorite spot on the mesa for his last breath and final goodbye. When the time came, they set up a bed in the back of his truck. Lily, Javier and his mom sat in back with Ethan, all covered in warm blankets, while Mac drove. Angie, Cleo, and Blue sat up front. Howard and Cindy followed with the chaises and more blankets.

Seven folding chaise lounges were set up next to each other. Ethan was between Lily and his father, who was next to his mother, then Javier next to Lily, then Cindy and Mac. Blue and Angie sat on a blanket next to Mac. Lily held the leash as Cleo lay on Ethan's chaise at his feet.

Norma and Alexa flew down a week later for the small ceremony to celebrate Ethan's life. Those who wanted to, spoke. Before ET was bedridden, he had placed a red earthen jar and lid, made years before, beside the Temple. Under it was a piece of paper on which he had written: Put my ashes in this please and place it where you want.

It was not clear who ET was directing, but after the ceremony Lily asked Becky and Howard to place it where they wanted. They chose right beside his studio door, looking out over the ranch.

Gotta Go Through It

Sadness and loss are everywhere. Ethan's absence permeates the soil, the trees, the sky and clouds. For now, Lily's grief is deep and wide, it can't be circumnavigated or ignored. When Mac tries to help her feel better, Lily says, with the dark, sunken eyes of plain old grief and not sleeping well, "This is how I feel. I need to live it, so please let me and don't worry."

Lily thought she was prepared, but she isn't. Her focus these past six months has been on ET and now she has to deal with herself again. She's angry at the world for taking ET so young. She spends days on end lying on a blanket under the cottonwood trees with Blue, Angie and Cleo beside her. Looking up to the sky or lying flat on her stomach feeling the earth beneath her belly, she asks the spirit of the earth to heal her.

Weeks later, when Lily has gone through the deepest part of her sadness and depression, she and Mac venture out for hikes, dinners, movies, and to their favorite church and sanctuary in Chimayo. They buy a little rhinestone bling collar for Cleo, dog treats for Angie and Blue, and jeans and shirts for themselves. One night Mac surprises Lily with a midnight-blue velvet Navajo skirt like the one the woman elder had worn, sitting in front of her hogan at Canyon de Chelly. It becomes Lily's signature clothing and she wears it almost every day.

In Santa Fe one day, they rent bikes and ride around town, going up Canyon Road, lined with galleries, then down around all the little streets where clothing, jewelry, restaurants and tourist shops are plentiful. When they are done, they walk to the plaza, where Mac is drawn to the intricate inlaid wood boxes a Navajo man is selling. Mac starts a conversation with the man and Lily goes to the bakery to pick up treats. When she returns, Mac is surrounded by the woodcarver and three other men, laughing and sharing stories as though they are longtime friends. Mac takes Lily's hand, introduces her to Henry and the other three, and tells her they invited him to join their card game, here in the plaza the following Tuesday.

With a big smile, Lily says, "That sounds fun. Nice to meet you all."

She loves how Mac draws people to him everywhere he goes. He's always interested in other people and is funny and kind, somewhat of a "life of the party" type person, though not the obnoxious kind. He's so comfortable with himself that he makes others feel comfortable too. There is a lightness and happiness about him that is contagious, yet he can be serious and quite thoughtful. Knowing he needs that kind of social interaction much more than she does, Lily says on their drive home, "Let's invite some of your work friends and anyone you want to the ranch for a Sunday brunch. That would be fun, and we can invite Cindy and Javier too, what do you think?"

Mac looks at Lily and smiles. "That would be great." Not a second later, he says, "Maybe I'll barbecue asparagus, eggplant, zucchini, onions, and other veggies, and make garlic bread."

"I can make a couple of quiches and brownies," Lily adds.

"We can offer beer and wine and ice tea. I can set up the table outside under the cottonwood trees. This is gonna be fun. Do you think two weeks from now?"

Lily happily smiles, "Yup."

That night after dinner, Mac gifts her a little inlaid wood box that Henry made.

The Naked Days

Eventually Lily and Mac brave entering ET's studio to clean up. The studio is immaculate, and in the middle of the room is a large, sheet-covered object. An attached note reads:

> Surprise, Lily! I made this for you when you bullied me to get back to work on small clay vessels. I delighted in hiding this from you and picturing your reaction right now! Blue has been your protector just as Cleo, in her way, has been mine. I know you and Mac will find the perfect spot to place him. I love you always, ET

Sitting on the floor, Lily cries, then she and Big Mac carry the life-size replica of Blue to the front porch and place it next to Blue's favorite spot, where the real Blue, between naps, looks down the driveway and watches over the ranch.

Mac and Lily had kept romance and sex on the down-low out of respect for ET. Now that it's just the two of them, they remember how attracted they are to each other. The weather has warmed, and one day out in the garden as they plant the early summer crops, one thing leads to the next and they find themselves hot, sweaty and naked in the freshly tilled soil. They spend much of the next few weeks running around the farm naked, enjoying each other's bodies.

One day Mac asks if Lily wants to have children.

"I don't know, for sure not yet, but maybe. You know I come with all kinds of parenting baggage. I am not sure if I see children in my life, but I definitely see our lives together."

The relief in Mac's face reminds Lily that she once left him and Norma without notice or thought. That night, lying in bed together, she puts her hand on his chest over his heart. "You know, Mac, I do love you. I may not show it very much sometimes because, well . . . I really don't know why, maybe I just forget. I do know for sure that I'm not a walk-away person any more. But I can't promise you now that I will want to have kids. It's a pretty scary thought to me. Will you be okay if we don't?"

"You are being a bit rough on yourself." He puts his arm around Lily's shoulders. "You show your love in different ways, by cooking for those you love and being there in a million ways. I hope you're done being a walk-away person. But I decided to trust you again, so let's just be honest and thoughtful with each other." He is silent for a moment. "If we have children, that would be great, but for now, let's see what the future brings."

Mac leaves for another six-week job in LA and Lily wanders around doing chores and taking Blue and Angie on well-traveled hiking paths. One day Howard and Becky stop by with sunflower seeds and other starts to plant near ET's urn. Afterward, the three of them light a candle and say silent prayers.

Touching Becky's hand, Lily says, "Ethan would have liked this. Thank you for being such good parents and raising a man like him."

Cottage Industry

Living on ET's ranch has become exactly what Lily wants, though she did not know this when she first arrived. It feels like she is starting a new life and she doesn't know exactly what that will be. Taking out her journal, Lily flips to the back and makes an outline of projects she has been thinking about, plus a money list. ET left her money to pay for ranch projects and upkeep, Mac tends to be generous, and she has Mother's monthly trust money; but Lily would like to earn enough money to pay for her own and the animals' everyday lives.

Her thoughts skip around to various ways of making money. Her first idea is to take her baked dog biscuits to a few pet boutiques in the area to see if they will sell. She has been playing with various biscuit recipes and has created one that lasts for weeks that the dogs love. She could make quilts and sell them, but all the hours that go into sewing one quilt mean that doesn't work financially. She considers a vegetable stand at the farmer's market, or maybe hand-sewn market bags, or fabric covers for dog beds that can be easily washed.

She likes these ideas and wants to let them sit in her mind for a while. She goes out to the glass house where ET slept the last weeks of his life. She, Blue, Angie, and Cleo started sleeping there when Mac left. Lying on the platform bed in the Temple of Heaven and Earth, Lily looks out the windows at the blue sky hanging above the trees and land until sleep befalls her.

During these days of being alone at the ranch, Lily hears on the radio that Amy Winehouse has died, overdosed on alcohol and who knows what else. Exactly Lily's age (well, two months older), she's dead at twenty-seven. Overcome with a grief that is not only about Amy, Lily slides into a funk and plays Amy's *Back to Black* CD for hours as she sings along. Knowing that she can't stay depressed and doesn't want to, she works in the garden and hangs out with the animals. Even the magpies intuitively come to visit. She calls Mac to hear his voice, calls Jonnie to catch up, and calls Norma to tell her the news. Norma says she'll come visit this weekend.

When Norma arrives, they only have three days together. On the drive from the airport to the ranch, Lily says, "I know you are wondering how I'm doing, so I'm going to say I'm okay. I think the worst is over. Of course I think of ET all the time and will always miss him, but I would not have given up my time with him for anything." Before Norma can answer, Lily continues, "ET was right. I love the house, the animals, and land here. This is my home now, I hope you are okay with that. Mac and I talked about building another house on the property for you and Alexa to come stay whenever you want, or maybe you will retire here."

Norma chuckles, "Well, I guess you answered my questions so I don't have to ask them. Retirement is a ways off and I still love Eagle Rock. Certainly Alexa and I will take holiday and summer vacations here. As a matter of fact, I hope it's okay if we come next year for all of August. We will probably travel around the Southwest, but you will be our home base."

"That sounds perfect. Is there anything in particular you want to do?"

"We have lots to talk about, that is number one, but I would like to go up to the Taos Pueblo, and I've heard there is a great flea market near here."

BLUE

I sleep on Norma's bed to keep her company. Late at night, Cleo joins us, her new diamond collar quite bright even at night. I haven't been able to take my eyes off it since she started wearing it. I guess I fell asleep because when I hear Norma get out of bed it is light already, that means breakfast. Lily puts my food bowl down first—still top dog—then she puts Angie's bowl on the other side of the kitchen. Angie slowly saunters over to her bowl. That dog is so slow to eat, I check every morning to see if she leaves any tasty morsels, but she never does.

• • • • • • •

The Rhinestone Collar

The Taos Pueblo is striking in simplicity and design. Lily and Norma walk around, thankful there are few tourists. The gray-brown of the buildings, the soil and the adobe exude silence, sadness, and an age-old hope. The feeling is powerful, and they sit silently beside the small stream that divides the central gathering place. A dry August wind moves the clouds overhead as chill air envelopes them. The weather in the high desert is so unpredictable, they think they might be caught in a rainstorm, so Norma and Lily hurry back to Homer to the rustling of aspen leaves singing loudly in the wind.

As they drive down the mountain to the Santa Fe Flea Market, the clouds clear and the sun shines brightly. Browsing tables and stalls, they stop at a crazily decorated shed and talk with the local artist who built it. Dried bones, plastic flowers, used paintbrushes, rubber and plastic dolls and rusted tools, along with his paintings, cover every inch of his studio shed. His work is eclectic, fanciful, very dark and yet full of life. Norma is drawn to his work and thinks he has probably traveled a very interesting road. She purchases a small painting of wild dogs in an otherworldly landscape, hoping Alexa will like it as much as she does.

Heading back through the market towards the car, Blue stops at a table. He jumps to put his front paws on the edge and grabs a belt on display. Lily says in a loud, strict voice, "Blue, what are you doing? Drop that!"

Blue drops it and sits as Lily picks up the belt and puts it back on the table, apologizing to the craftswoman. Lily and Norma walk away but Blue stays where he is, sitting by the artist's booth. Lily says, "Blue! Come on, what are you doing?"

Blue's eyes are fixed on the turquoise-dyed leather belt with large, shining rhinestones. Norma says, "I think Blue wants that belt! It looks like a big version of Cleo's collar."

"Oh. My. God!" Lily breaks into laughter. She picks up the belt and asks Blue, "Do you want a glam diamond collar like Cleo's?"

Blue bangs his body against Lily and wiggles every which way.

In awe, Norma says, "That dog is the smartest animal I have ever met. I'm going to buy him that belt, and we can take it to a leather repair shop and have it made into a collar to fit his neck." She pays the craftswoman and thanks her as she places the belt in a brown bag and hands it to Blue, who carries the bag proudly in his mouth as they walk to the car.

BLUE

We stop at a shoe repair shop on the way home and I wait while the man measures my neck and turns the rhinestone belt into a collar for me. Norma puts it on me and I catch a glimpse of my new sparkling self in the full-length mirror. I look amazing! I turn sideways as Norma and Lily smile and laugh.

Norma says, "Blue, I think you are the canine reincarnation of Elvis."

I wiggle my body. I can't wait to show off to Cleo. I look more handsome than ever!

• • • • • • •

Little Clay Bowls

Norma leaves and Lily is alone with the animals for a couple more weeks, before Mac comes back from working in The Angels. She takes up her journal writing again.

> *I used to think that we create our own stories, but now I believe that our lives are already known within ourselves, we just have to listen and learn from the inside out. Maybe, like an unfinished book, the story is there; we just choose the adverbs, adjectives, verbs, and nouns, and our attitude modifies the story.*
>
> *After Father's visit last Christmas, I see him now as just another adult with his allotted frailties and compulsions. He is selfish and obviously thinks women are here only for his benefit. My poor birth mother, and Mother. Why would Mother, so talented in her own right, be with a man like that? Both Mother and Father seemed*

so lost to themselves, and obviously they never wanted to look inside.

I have no idea what drove my birth mother, Gwen, to kill herself. She was so young, that is incredibly sad. I am older now than she was when she died. One day I will try to find out more about her. There should be a record of her at Occidental when she was a grad student, but I am not ready to do that yet. For some reason I have never wanted to know about her. Maybe loss is woven into my DNA. Maybe in writing this, I am getting prepared to find out more. I don't know, time will tell.

There's been too much death in my life. I feel it today. Sometimes it seems like death comes and shakes me so hard my feet can't find the ground. If I didn't have the dogs and Cleo, I think I could just float away. I need to crawl back into my earthling body again, to bury my hands deep in the soil right now and plant the new raised vegetable bed Mac built. I'll let the goats and chickens out to wander the property, they help bring me back to earth.

Reading over her list of moneymaking ideas, Lily adds decorative dog bowls to the list. She decides to give it a try, as her dog biscuits, displayed in silly or cute-looking ceramic dog food bowls, may sell.

At first Lily just plays around with the clay stored in ET's studio. It feels weird, but a good weird, to be working where he worked for so many years. She rolls out flat slabs of porcelain clay exactly like she does with flour dough for making pies, then bends and presses them into bowl shapes. She cuts out clay shapes like ET did and adheres them to the outside of the bowls. With a pointed wooden tool, she carves lines and scrolls into the clay. Her pieces look small, childish and basic, but she likes them and thinks they will be perfect for small dogs like the Chihuahua mixes that are so popular. Laughing at her vision of hundreds of Chihuahuas eating out of her bowls, she acknowledges that she is enjoying working with the clay.

She calls Javier and asks if he knows how to work the kiln. He does, and he and Cindy come that Saturday. Besides working the kiln, Lily learns a few carving and glazing techniques that Javier absorbed over the years of hanging out with ET in the studio. A couple of weeks later, Lily takes a half dozen dog bowls and bagged dog biscuits to her favorite designer dog food store. They buy all she has and order another dozen. At the bookstore, Lily purchases a how-to ceramic book and starts playing with new bowl designs. She has discovered her small business for the time being, and decides to name it Extra Terrestrial, to honor ET's memory.

On his way back from work, Mac catches a nasty cold on the airplane. His decline into sickness is like a huge redwood tree cruelly chopped down. Always so strong and resilient, Lily learns that Mac is a whole other type of creature when he is sick. He can barely talk and when he does, he is a complete grouch. Lily makes a special spiced soup and tries to take care of him but realizes it's best to keep her distance from his bad mood.

When she calls his mother for tips, Pam responds, "Oh Lily, you poor thing! Marty can be so awful when he is sick, give him a wide berth. Really, just leave him alone. When he starts to feel better his mood will lighten, and you will recognize him again."

In a way, it's a relief for Lily to learn that Mac is not perfect.

· · ·

Jonnie comes to stay, as she and Heather have had an ugly breakup. Lily likes having Jonnie at the ranch and says she can stay as long as she likes. Their days are spent taking Blue and Angie to explore every river, mesa and mountain in the area. Infatuated with the high desert and seeing a lifestyle that suits her, Jonnie decides to apply for a job at the local animal shelter. If she gets it, she will move here. Lily is ecstatic just thinking about it.

After a couple days together, nearly forgetting that she has not told Jonnie yet, Lily shares the story of what happened on the Gualala River. In the way only Jonnie can, she says, "Damn, girl, I had no idea you were so tough under your hippie-dippy exterior. And Blue, my boy, is the best damn dog I have ever met."

The Way It Is

On certain nights at sunset, it looks like someone tossed handfuls of silver coins across the swirling lavender and pink clouds, and it feels like heartbreak or reignited love. Other times, as the sun slips and dives behind the mountains, a cold and bitter harshness fills the air. Either way, Lily is in awe of this high desert landscape. It's December once again and the skies are full of every human emotion.

Lily's twenty-eighth birthday and Christmas are both coming up, and she is in the midst of making holiday gifts and decorations. Getting ET's sewing machine out again, Lily decides to make grocery shopping bags for everyone. She sets up the dining table with scrap clothes from the closets, including many of ET's shirts and pants plus pieces she has picked up from the Goodwill, and gets to work making these recycled patchwork bags.

Mac is working a lot on a new TV series filming in New Mexico and seems to be traveling all over the state. Jonnie loves her job at the animal shelter, where Lily now volunteers three half-days a week. Between this, taking care of the ranch, and making bowls and biscuits for her growing Extra Terrestrial business, Lily is happily busy. Howard and Becky are traveling in Europe. From their sporadic emails, they seem to be trying to start new lives. Howard is taking cooking classes in Rome and Becky is studying European art history, visiting galleries and museums.

Lily misses Ethan, but she knows that is just the way it is. Working on her ceramic bowls a few days a week, it seems that he is whispering encouragement in her ear, and new ideas magically percolate in her head. Her home-baked dog biscuits and bowls are selling well at a number of stores in Santa Fe and Taos.

Celebrating a low-key Christmas along with Lily's birthday, the extended family group enjoys a casual breakfast. There are fresh eggs, bagels, tomatoes, yogurt, and California avocados and lemons that Norma and Alexa bring from their garden in Eagle Rock. Afterwards, Jonnie, Javier, Cindy, Alexa, Norma, Lily, Big Mac, Blue and Angie hike the Gorge Trail, which seems to have become a ritual.

The air is extremely dry and cold and the frozen ground makes crackling noises with each step. Wrapped in sweaters, jackets and warm scarves, they walk in silence. Mountain and sky spirits whisper stories of each leaf and wisp of cloud. Halfway to the gorge,

Lily stops on the trail to let the group walk ahead. Blue stays behind with her and she hugs him big, calling him her prince of princes, king of kings. Blue smiles his goofy smile and wags his tail, his turquoise and rhinestone collar shimmering in the sunshine. Stretching her arms out wide to the sky, she asks Yah to bless them all, including Ethan's spirit.

At the Rio Grande overlook, Javier says, "I feel like ET is with us today." They all agree and reminisce about last year's Christmas. Not much else is said as they traipse back up the trail at a snail's pace, honoring Blue's need to go slow. Mac lifts Blue into the car, where he and Angie are wrapped in blankets on their beds. Lily straightens Blue's bling collar and snowflake-patterned sweater, understanding that this will be his last time hiking the Gorge Trail. He is exhausted.

Losing Blue is almost unthinkable. Lily remembers finding him, all those years ago. He has been her life's touchstone for the last nine years. He has practically raised her; he has been her confidant, protector, moneymaker, savior and joy. Lily knows for sure that she doesn't want him to live in pain or to die during a seizure, which she has learned can happen. She watches him closely.

Blue sleeps a lot these days, and sometimes doesn't wake even when Lily shakes the car keys. In the past he would hear the slightest jingle and bound to the door, wriggling and wagging, ready for adventure. With hearing and sight now diminished, he meanders, zig-zags, and even waddles his way through the world.

He is not in pain, as he is on medication for arthritis, but since the end of the warm weather it seems that each month he grows older and more tired.

Lily is grateful that Jonnie is here; she will be able to read the signs better than anyone. Jonnie says that dogs who have been abused as puppies, like Blue was before Lily found him, usually don't live as long as dogs who have not been abused. Lily knows that the time in Santa Cruz when she didn't care for him well enough took a toll on his body, as did the attack on the Gualala River. Blue used a lot of his life energy to save them both.

BLUE

I hear a little sound, is it part of my dream? I don't know, so I snooze a bit more. I feel a soft pat on my neck and smell a slight fragrance of roses and lavender. It's Lily. She has my leash in her hand, which means we get to go for a walk. I hop up as best I can and trot to the front door, which is already open. There is snow on the ground and Lily puts my sweater on.

These days Lily takes me for our private "love walks" at least twice a day. They are short, but Lily talks with me and touches me a lot on these walks. Recently I am getting a bit confused. I think I am going into Lily and Mac's bedroom, then find myself in the living room. Usually Lily, Jonnie, or Mac come and get me. The only place I'm not confused is in the kitchen. My eyes may be dim and my hearing impaired, but my nose still works excellently. Lily feeds me all kinds of treats every day: hamburgers, just like I loved at the restaurant in Santa Cruz, including the secret sauce; turkey hot dogs; sliced cheese; and fresh, crunchy romaine lettuce that Lily calls "palate cleansers." My favorite is when Lily has a vanilla ice cream cone and says, "Blue, let's share this."

I take a lick, a pretty big one, then Lily licks a little from the side of the cone, then my turn again. This time I take a huge lick, and Lily laughs and calls me her little piglet as she brings the cone back to my lips. Then she asks, "Can you eat any more, or should I throw it away?"

I nod my head, of course I can eat more. I may be old but I'm not crazy! As the last of the cool, creamy sweetness slides down my throat, I get to nibble on the crispy cone. It's a whole process, with Lily turning the cone slowly in her hand as I only use my front teeth to take little tiny bites. Lily taught me how to do this when we lived in Santa Cruz. Sometimes after performing on the street, she would buy us an ice cream cone to share. I remember people putting money in Midas just for watching us eat ice cream!

· · · · · · ·

Christmas break is nearly over, and before Norma leaves to go back to work in LA, she asks Lily to come with her to buy a turquoise ring as a surprise for Alexa. She has a sneaking suspicion that Alexa bought her a secret gift as well, as she saw her pack a small box. Norma tells Lily that she and Alexa want to have a commitment ceremony early next summer in Eagle Rock.

Without being asked, Lily jumps in and says, "OMG, this is so exciting! Mac and I will be there! We are invited, right?"

"Of course, and I would love if you stood for me, which means being my maid of honor."

"Yes! Thank you, Norma, I would be honored."

Later in the day, Norma asks Lily if she will be all right after Blue goes.

"Really, I don't know. Jonnie says to start getting ready, even though Blue is still happy and enjoying his life. I know it will be the hardest thing in my life. Harder even than letting go of Ethan . . . or killing that man. When the time comes, I want you, Jonnie, Mac and me to surround Blue, as we have been the four pillars that hold up the sky for him. You'll come, won't you?"

"Of course, and I'll stay as long as you need me. Afterwards, you will need to keep very busy. Blue is so interwoven into every moment of your every day, I can't even imagine. At least Angelica has become a good companion. You have done a great job with her."

"Thanks, Norma. I may need you to stay awhile, but I don't know. I have an idea I've discussed with Mac about starting a dog rescue when Blue dies. I think the best way to honor Blue's life is to help save other dogs. Mac loves the idea, and it will be easy with Jonnie working at the shelter, as she can test temperament. Also, when I turn thirty, Mother's trust will be mine. I don't know how much it will be, but I'm sure it will help with advertising and supplies as the rescue grows."

Lily's voice becomes more animated. "You know, even as a puppy, Blue probably would never have been adopted, with his scars and big head and wide jaw. The shelters can't do it all, and I think Mac and Jonnie and I can create something really positive. Mother might roll in her grave, putting her money toward saving animals; I don't think she ever met an animal that wasn't cooked and on her plate. But truthfully, I am so thankful that Mother was kind enough to leave me this money, something I would never have thought she would do. Jonnie and I are thinking we'll offer small adoption fairs at the ranch one Sunday a month. I am thinking of calling it 'Blue's Rescue.' What do you think?"

"I love the idea. Maybe Alexa and I can help in some way. I'm pretty sure we will want to adopt a dog in the next year or so."

Prince of Princes, King of Kings

Lily, Mac, Cleo and the dogs move into ET's larger bedroom, where there's more space for the dog beds and Cleo's climbing condo. There's a door to the outside so Blue can easily do his business. Mac and Lily paint the walls a buttery yellow and change some of the furniture.

They are nesting again, and it feels right. Mac is getting more TV and film jobs in Albuquerque, so he is home more often. Lily's business is booming and she is often in the studio with Blue, Angie and Cleo sleeping next to her work table. This and That, the magpies, sometimes pop in on their way to forage in the garden and around the property. Since summer, Lucinda and Gladys, the chickens, and Simon the goat have died, joining Frank, Barbara, Jacqueline and Pearl near the vegetable garden in the animal cemetery ET created years ago. Living with animals, Lily has learned that every now and then there will be another burial. Linda is the only goat left, and Annette, the only chicken. They are good friends so they're not lonely, but Lily makes sure they get lots of attention and special treats. It is clear their days are numbered as well. Mac and Lily have decided they won't get any more goats, but they may adopt a few rescue chickens.

Jonnie has moved into her own place in Santa Fe. She is dating a variety of women and is not in any hurry to settle down with one person. Her shelter job is almost perfect, and her goal is to one day become the shelter director.

• • •

Today is the first anniversary of ET's death. The mountains are in full view and the cottonwood trees sprout green foliage, the land once again taking shape in early spring. Lily places fresh flowers at ET's altar outside his studio, lights candles and says a prayer of thanks to him.

On April 16 they celebrate ET's birthday. Javier and Cindy come over, along with Jonnie and her latest girlfriend, Ina. The day is warm, so they move the long table that ET and Mac made out to the garden and have a big picnic as ET's favorite music plays in the background. Blue lies in the sun on the warm dry ground, his bling collar glittering in the sunshine. Angie and Cleo lie right next to him. These days they have become Blue's guides, especially at night, when they lead him from room to room so he doesn't bang into walls.

Lily often whispers to Blue that she will be fine when he's ready to cross the Rainbow Bridge, and that ET will be waiting for him. She leans right close to his ear and says, "Don't worry about protecting me anymore. You have been my amazing best friend and have done the best job any dog could do. You will be with me forever, my prince of princes, my king of kings. You will always live in my heart."

Seeing Blue's life slipping, Mac asks Lily where she wants to bury him. They walk the whole property, looking at each location, and Lily decides on the sunniest spot, next to Ethan's Temple of Heaven and Earth. She will plant a tree where Blue's body will be interred. After research, Lily decides on a golden rain tree, a deciduous tree with beautiful burnt-orange fall leaves, delicate yellow flowers that attract bees, and paper-like lantern seed pods that hang from the branches for much of the winter.

Mac is worried. He knows that Lily is doing what she can to prepare, but how can someone get ready to lose their "one true thing"? That special being protected Lily, loved her unconditionally, has been her constant companion and confidant, and for a while was her only reason to live. Lily and Mac very much love each other, but there is no love or devotion like that of a dog like Blue. Mac tears up every time he thinks of Blue dying. He knows this will be a tsunami of sadness. When Lily is ready, he will take her on a trip somewhere she has never been. She has talked about wanting to visit Oaxaca, Mexico. Jonnie will stay at the ranch and care for the animals.

One month and a year after Ethan's death, the veterinarian comes to the ranch to help Blue pass peacefully. It's time. Due to his medication he's not in any pain, but for two days Mac and Lily have carried him and held him to go potty. He doesn't want to eat much and only takes few small licks of the vanilla ice cream cones Lily offers.

Angie and Cleo are inside the house, as they will be upset if they are close by. Mac carries Blue to place him on his blanketed bed, which Lily put outside on his favorite patch of dirt by the front porch, where the sun shines on him. Norma, Jonnie and Mac sit on the ground surrounding Blue, and Lily sits with Blue's head lying gently on her lap. The veterinarian gives Blue a tranquilizer shot to make sure he is thoroughly relaxed. Looking only at Blue, their tears flowing, everyone rests their hands gently on Blue's body. Lily bends over to whisper in Blue's ear, "My prince of princes, my king of kings. Thank you for taking such good care of me and loving me. I love you, Blue."

Blue looks into Lily's eyes, licks her hand one last time, and falls to sleep. The vet waits a few minutes, then administers the euthanasia shot.

BLUE

I see Lily and lick her hand as she calls me her prince, her king. The light gets really bright and I am running full speed. Lily is very close, next to me, laughing and jumping in the air. My body is strong and we are bounding across the mesa. My legs

stretch and pull, and my ears feel happy as they flap in the breeze. The air smells like bouquets of lavender and roses. My heart is pounding. I smile big at Lily, and she laughs and kisses me as together we run into the light.

. . . .

Acknowledgements

Thank you to my incredible writing sisters: Karen Sallovitz, Mary Camille Thomas, Sarojani Rohan, Kim Woodland, Lea Haratani, Maggie Muir and Kat Brown, and to Carolyn Flynn and her writing groups. Their care, support and enthusiasm throughout this process has made all the difference.

Thank you to Melody Culver, my trusted editor and to Tor Anderson, cover designer.

Thank you always to my wonderful family, and to my circle of friends and loved ones.

To all the dogs who have trained me and shared their lives with me, including Gretchen, who I found in a garbage bin when I was nineteen and who helped raise me. To Cowboy the basset hound, the funniest dog I ever met, who loved entertaining us with his version of the moonwalk. To Wesley, my extra-large gentle giant with a heart of gold, who helped me foster and train many a rescue. To Mary-Margaret, my beloved bloodhound, who rarely listened to the rules and was completely loved anyway. And to The Captain, my prince of princes, one of the kindest and most true-blue creatures ever.

To name a few more wonderful rescue dogs: Jonathan, Martha, Jane, Professor, Yoda, Savannah, Dahlilah, Aunt Bea, David, Lincoln, Justice, Rebecca, Annabelle, and Alice, my son's wonderful rescue dog.

And to the cats, Cleo and Simon; and to the chickens, Naomi and June.

I am forever blessed to have had all of you in my life.